D0965573

KILLER, COME HITHER

ALSO BY LOUIS BEGLEY

FICTION

Memories of a Marriage

Schmidt Steps Back

Matters of Honor

Shipwreck

Schmidt Delivered

Mistler's Exit

About Schmidt

As Max Saw It

The Man Who Was Late

Wartime Lies

NONFICTION

Why the Dreyfus Affair Matters

Franz Kafka: The Tremendous World I Have Inside My Head

Killer, Come Hither

LOUIS BEGLEY

Nan A. Talese | DOUBLEDAY

NEW YORK LONDON TORONTO SYDNEY AUCKLAND

All rights reserved. Published in the United States by
Nan A. Talese / Doubleday, a division of Random House LLC,
New York, and in Canada by Random House of Canada, Limited,
Toronto, Penguin Random House companies.

www.nanatalese.com

Doubleday is a registered trademark of Random House LLC.
Nan A. Talese and the colophon are trademarks of Random
House LLC.

Jacket design Michael J. Windsor
Jacket images: mouse trap © bikeriderlondon/Shutterstock;
landscape © Ann Jacobson Photography/Moment Open/Getty
Images

Library of Congress Cataloging-in-Publication Data
Begley, Louis.
   Killer, come hither : a novel / Louis Begley. — First edition.
      pages ; cm
      ISBN 978-0-385-53914-2 (hardcover : acid-free paper)
978-0-385-53915-9 (eBook) 1. Authors—Fiction. 2. Murder—
Investigation—Fiction. 3. Billionaires—Fiction.
4. Corporations—Currupt practices—Fiction. I. Title.
   PS3552.E373K55   2015
   813'.54—dc23   2014018447

MANUFACTURED IN THE UNITED STATES OF AMERICA

10 9 8 7 6 5 4 3 2 1
First Edition

For Anka, this departure

KILLER, COME HITHER

I

This is a true story. I have changed the names of certain persons in order to protect them from harm. Other than that, I have concealed nothing. My conscience is clear. What I've done I'd do again without a moment's hesitation. Some will think that I should have stuck to the rules—put my faith in criminal justice and let the murderer plea-bargain his way to a cushy sentence. So be it. I despise cowards and hypocritical pussies, and their holier-than-thou naïveté.

My name is Jack Dana. I am a former Marine Infantry officer and Force Recon platoon leader. I am also the author of three successful books. The first of these I wrote at Walter Reed, undergoing surgeries to fix the damage done to my pelvis by the bullets of a Taliban sniper outside Delaram (a nasty spot in Afghanistan's Helmand Province) in the minute or so before my team killed him. It may seem odd that someone like me—honor graduate of the Corps' toughest combat schools, those where you learn to gun down enemies unlucky enough to be in range or, if they're close enough, punch a blade between their ribs—should become a novelist. The truth is that to every thing there is a season. I put my training to use during deployments to Iraq and Afghanistan, and in the door-to-door fighting in the second battle for Fallujah I learned how easy it is to kill a man. You squeeze the trigger slowly; the round finds its target, and he crumples and falls to the ground. Easier yet, you throw a satchel charge through a window, and down comes the building. I would have gone on doing just that but, though the repairs of which the surgeons were so proud had put me into excellent shape, my new excellent wasn't good enough for a Corps Infantry officer. Never mind. Writing books was a return of sorts to the life I expected to lead before we were attacked on September 11, 2001.

I am the only child of a Harvard philosophy professor father and a flutist mother who played with a Boston-based chamber orchestra, and I was raised in a comfortable clapboard house off Brattle Street in Cambridge, Massachusetts. After graduating from a New Hampshire boarding school that my father and his younger only sibling, Harry, had also attended, I went to Yale. Why Yale instead of Harvard, my father's and uncle's alma mater? I didn't want to be in my father's ample shadow. For the same reason, while I planned to pursue an academic career, I shied away from philosophy, choosing instead ancient Greek and Roman history. Alas, before long I was to regret bitterly the decision that had taken me away from Cambridge. My beautiful and gifted mother fell sick during the spring of my freshman year. By the following Christmas she was dead, the victim of a furiously aggressive ovarian cancer. My father's despair knew no bounds. I went up to see him on as many weekends as I could, but my efforts to help him shake off depression were mostly unavailing. He had never fully recovered from wounds and other traumas he'd suffered during the fighting in Vietnam. A massive stroke felled him in the winter of my senior year. Paralyzed from the neck down, he slipped into a vegetative coma, and it took all of Uncle Harry's calm authority and legal skill to get the hospital to respect my father's health directive and my wishes and disconnect him from life-support machines. We buried him alongside my mother in the Mount Auburn Cemetery.

My mother had been an only child. Uncle Harry, now my only living relative, had never married and considered me the son he would have wished to have. Lest one draw unwarranted inferences or buy into the slurs that have been spread about him, I affirm that he was anything but gay—closeted or otherwise. But he'd been unlucky in love, attaching himself to married women who in the end could not bring themselves to leave their cuckolded husbands, and, in one case, to a woman who put her career ahead of him. She was a famous ballerina who had told him from the first that she didn't think marriage and her art could be reconciled. Gradually, they drifted apart. His last great love was a much-younger Peruvian lawyer, a raven-haired beauty who laid claim to Inca blood. They met in Lima where she assisted him, as Peruvian local counsel, in the negotiation of a copper mine investment by Harry's client, Abner Brown. The reclusive and eccentric

Texas billionaire was not yet generally known to the American public as the embodiment of extreme right-wing politics. Harry had begun working for him a year or so earlier, having been recommended by a satisfied client. Harry was a man of perfect manners and unbending principles. Mixing professional dealings with romance was taboo so far as he was concerned, and he was convinced that his courtship of Olga began only at the barbecue Brown gave at his ranch outside Houston to celebrate the successful closing of the Peruvian transaction, which, he said in toasting Harry, had added a cool five hundred million dollars to his fortune. Harry, he gloated, took those Peruvian bureaucratic monkeys to the cleaners, ha! ha! ha! Fortunately, none of those scorned monkeys was present. Indeed, the only Peruvian in attendance was Olga. In the course of apologizing to her for Brown's odious tirade, Harry discovered to his astonishment and joy that she hadn't thought of being angry at him, and that she had seen through his carefully maintained policy of injecting no personal feelings into their professional relationship: his suit had been expected and was welcome. It did not take them long to decide they would be married as soon as Olga had completed work on her pending legal cases or transferred them to other lawyers in her firm. They planned a Lima wedding in September of 1992. Fate had other plans. Olga was one of the twenty-odd victims killed by a truck-bomb attack launched in July of that year by the Shining Path insurgency in what became known, after the street down which the truck rolled, as the Tarata bombing. A week of violent attacks followed, paralyzing Lima. The capture of Shining Path's supreme leader, Abimael Guzmán, two months later knocked the wind out of the insurgency's sails, but that was no consolation to my uncle. He considered himself a widower and spent the rest of his life mourning his lost Inca.

My Christmas and spring vacation trips to visit Harry, which I made alone as soon as I went to boarding school, were treats to which I looked forward all through the school year. He practiced law in Manhattan as a leading corporate partner in the powerful Jones & Whetstone firm. His apartment on Fifth Avenue was steps away from the Metropolitan Museum. At his urging, I explored its galleries, sometimes accompanied by a young curator. Harry knew everybody, and that sort of thing seemed easy for him to arrange. In the evening—and whenever he was free at lunch—he'd invite me to his club or to one of the French restaurants he liked best. Other evenings we went to the opera, theater, or ballet, and it's no exaggeration to say that Harry formed my taste in art and music. There were also family visits. Those had usually taken place in the summer, when my parents and he were all on vacation. We'd spend a long weekend at his Long Island home in the part of Sag Harbor that escaped the conflagration of 1845, which destroyed much of that once-important port. His house was an early-nineteenth-century structure, a warren of small rooms, many of them strangely shaped, complemented by a barn that had been converted into a high-ceilinged studio with its own bathroom. The studio was officially Harry's office, but when I was finally allowed to visit him in Sag Harbor alone he told me to consider it my bedroom and my private domain. As it turned out, however,

I hardly ever slept in it after that first summer. I preferred to be in the guest bedroom across the corridor from Harry's bedroom and realized he rather liked his postprandial naps on the sofa in the studio.

That our family visits to Sag Harbor were never longer, in spite of the comfort of Harry's house and the allure of his sailboat and the bay and ocean beaches, was due to the tension between him and my father. On the surface, their relationship was as affectionate as befit two brothers separated in age by not more than three years, and the difficulty was never alluded to by them. But it was there: a black storm cloud visible in a brilliant summer sky. The explanation was given to me by my mother, the person who was closest to Harry, at a time when she knew she was dying. She wanted me to understand both him and my father better. The rift—for it was really that, not a quarrel—could be traced to Harry's not having served during the Vietnam War. He had waited for the draft board to call him up and in the course of the pre-induction medical examination was classified 4F on a basis he never disclosed. Since he was an avid, expert, and indefatigable swimmer and tennis player, it seemed inconceivable that he had been turned down on account of a physical condition. Had the psychiatric part of the exam revealed a psychosis that had gone until then unnoticed? Or had he, as my father and grandfather suspected but would never say, led the doctor to the erroneous—of that they were convinced—conclusion that he was gay? It didn't matter. Since he had not expressed an insurmountable objection to the war, their own conclusion, intolerable to my warrior father and his and

Harry's warrior father, was that Harry had weaseled out of serving, that he was a coward. My mother didn't care. All that mattered to her was the conviction that Harry had a heart of gold and could be trusted to look after my welfare.

Indeed, I cannot imagine what would have become of me without Harry during the dreadful spring when my father was dying. His steady and unobtrusive help let me keep my emotional balance and complete my senior year's work successfully enough to graduate with highest honors and be awarded a Yale scholarship for study at Balliol College at Oxford. All the tasks connected with closing and selling my parents' house and settling my father's estate were likewise lifted from my shoulders, so that once again I was able to concentrate on my studies. The result was far beyond my hopes. Just before Easter, I was invited to join the Society of Fellows at Harvard as a Junior Fellow. It was an academic honor with important practical implications. The stipend I would receive during the following three academic years would allow me to pursue my studies in my own way, without the need to enroll in a Ph.D. program or to start looking immediately for a teaching position. I would be free to find my own way. Harry was the trustee of the small trust my father had set up for me under his will. I wrote to him about the Society of Fellows and asked whether he thought I could afford a four-to-six-week summer vacation in Italy. With a guest, I specified, an English girl I'd met at Oxford and hoped to convince to do graduate work at Harvard. Harry's answer came by phone. After he had finally finished congratulating me, he gave me his answer: Money isn't a problem, but the canicular heat will be. Don't be a cheapskate and make sure you and the young lady are at the beach or have access to a swimming pool.

Directly after Labor Day, I flew from Rome to Boston and went about organizing my new life in Cambridge, my lovely Felicity having promised to join me during her winter break. I thought we'd surprise Harry by spending Christmas with him and then try powder-snow skiing in Alta. To my delight, the small apartment on Craigie Street that the university had recommended was exactly what I wanted. I signed the lease, arranged to have some pieces of my parents' furniture delivered from storage, and had electricity and telephone and Internet service turned on. Then on September 10, I took the shuttle to LaGuardia and went straight to Harry's office, getting there by midafternoon, to wish him a happy birthday. Making a fuss was a better decision than I had realized. His secretary had given him a present—cuff links, he showed me—and a couple of younger partners he worked with had taken him to lunch at a sushi restaurant, but he had no plans for the evening.

It's my own decision, he told me. My law school classmate and best friend at the firm, Simon Lathrop, and his wife wanted to have a small dinner, but I wasn't up to it. Olga and I were going to be married this very weekend, nine years ago. Spending the evening with four or five apparently happy couples . . . I just couldn't do it. Even if some of them are people I genuinely love. That's why I usually celebrate my birthday by getting away. But this week and the next I'm stuck in the city. I should tell you that I had another, special reason for not accepting the Lathrops' invitation. I was secretly hoping you'd show up.

My present consisted of taking Harry out to dinner. It being Monday evening, his favorite French restaurant was closed, and I told him that if we were to have a meal up to his standards he had better pick a replacement.

There is an Italian restaurant I like a lot, he said, that serves food from the Trieste region. If you're not sick and tired of Italian food, let's go there.

We met at the restaurant and treated the dinner with the seriousness it merited, finishing off a bottle of old Barolo and lingering after the meal over a single varietal grappa. It was past eleven when we left the restaurant. To clear our heads, an effort that in my case didn't entirely succeed, we walked the twenty-odd blocks to Harry's apartment. At some point mild inebriation gave me the necessary courage, and I asked whether he had really decided to live out his life alone. Could it be that his love for Olga excluded the possibility of another attachment? He was silent for a long while, and I feared that I had made him angry. His answer reassured me.

It's not that simple, he told me. Olga wouldn't have wanted me to be so lonely. But something like a wall of ice has built up around me, and it's harder and harder to break a passage through it. Strangely, finding my work as satisfying as I do, having deep relationships with people in the firm, especially younger partners and associates who work for me, liking my clients, have had a perverse effect, reinforcing my isolation. My igloo is very comfortable! And don't forget, there is also my adorable Plato. . . .

I had to smile at that, and to conceal my delight. Plato was Harry's Burmese kitten, a tomcat almost small enough to hold in my rather-large hand when I gave him to Harry for his birthday a year ago, just before flying off to England. It turned out to be love at first sight and had only grown more solid. Letters and emails brought me news of Plato's exploits—in the New York apartment they played an elaborate game of marbles, Harry rolling them to Plato and Plato batting them back with his paw, and in Sag Harbor, once Harry decided he could allow Plato the run of the garden, the kitty proved to be a redoubtable hunter, the scourge of mice and chipmunks—and ever since Harry had learned to email photos, he circulated images of Plato with the pride of a new father. I had spent only a few hours with Plato that afternoon, but, having been brought up with cats, I didn't need more to be conquered once again by the little fellow's intelligence and elegant manners.

We said good night as soon as we got home. Harry told me that he had to be at the office early and would be leaving the apartment before eight. He didn't expect that I'd be awake or that he'd see me at breakfast. If I were you I'd get a real night's sleep. I'm having lunch with a client, he added, so you're on your own during the day, and the ballet and the opera seasons haven't begun, but it's my turn to take you to dinner. At my French restaurant if that suits you.

That suited me just fine, but plans, both trivial and weighty, were upended, and the texture of the days, months, and years that followed was irremediably changed when next morning four hijacked planes toppled the North and South Towers of the World Trade Center, plowed into the western side of the Pentagon, and crashed in a field near Shanksville, Pennsylvania. I had followed Harry's advice and gotten up late and was having my first cup of coffee when the telephone rang. It was Harry, telling me to turn on the TV. A couple of hours later he called again and said his office was closing. He would walk home along Fifth Avenue. We agreed I'd meet him halfway.

The next day, Wednesday, was when I had intended to leave, but flights had been canceled across the nation, and trains weren't running. I remained at Harry's apartment, glued to the television. A conviction had grown by the evening that Osama bin Laden, a name I had never heard before, was responsible for the attacks; he had commissioned and masterminded them from his lair somewhere in Afghanistan. There were reports of explosions in Kabul, but the Pentagon denied rumors that we had attacked the city. Harry and I had dinner at his French restaurant. We ate the postponed grand meal, drinking too much, and both of us feeling we were at a wake. When I mentioned the explosions, Harry said that even if it were true that we had not yet moved against bin Laden we'd be doing so soon.

You heard Bush, he continued, hunt them down and punish, making no distinction between those who committed the acts of terror and those who harbor and support them. That's quite a brief! Lord knows what the country will get into. Look, he added after a pause, it doesn't seem to me that you need to try to move heaven and earth to be in Cambridge tomorrow or any other day this week. You aren't teaching or taking courses you shouldn't miss. Why not stay here until things quiet down? Having you with me is a wonderful serendipity. It may not be repeated. I want to take the good with the bad.

I agreed gratefully.

The drumbeat of war continued implacably all that week, gaining in force. Colin Powell issued his own warning to foreign nations: You're with us or against us. NATO invoked the common defense clause of the treaty, laying the ground for intervention. A couple of days later President Bush promised to lead the world to victory and declared that states that support terrorism would be "ended." Reading the press compulsively, I came across an article filed by Tony Lewis, a *New York Times* columnist, that spoke bluntly about the president's inexperience in war and statecraft and the danger that retaliatory action by the U.S. would trigger unintended consequences—such as those that followed from our arming the mujahideen fighting the Soviets in Afghanistan in 1979 and the early eighties. We woke up to find we had handed over that country to anti-Western extremists. But his was a voice crying in the wilderness. On September 14, Congress passed a resolution allowing the president to attack nations, organizations, and persons suspected of being involved in the 9/11 terrorist acts, or harboring such organizations and persons, and to prevent future acts of terror by such nations, organizations, or persons. The House voted for it 420 to 1; the Senate 98 to 0. The ground had been well prepared: a national poll taken the following Monday showed overwhelming public support for military action.

Harry worked at the office during that first post-9/11 weekend. The weather being beautiful, I divided my time between Central Park and the Metropolitan Museum. In reality, wherever I was I brooded about the impending war, my chosen work—a revisionist study of the Athenian campaign in Sicily—that awaited me in Cambridge and that I was eager to complete, my family history, and the moral quandary I faced. By the time my father was my age, the pace of the Vietnam War had picked up. Conscription was in effect. When the notice from the draft board came, you had to report for duty unless you had secured a deferment or had avoided the issue by joining the National Guard or, like Harry, had been deemed unfit for service. My father didn't wait to be drafted. Far from seeking a deferment for graduate studies—he had already been accepted by the Harvard graduate school and a deferment would have been his for the asking—upon graduation from Harvard College he applied for a commission in the Marine Corps and was accepted for training. As platoon leader and eventually company commander, he took part in some of the most vicious fighting of the Vietnam War, including the Battle of Khe Sanh. For bravery in that action he was awarded the Navy Cross; he had previously received the Silver Star. He had not had any particular desire to fight in Vietnam; although he loved France, he had deplored her colonial policy and thought it was a mistake for the U.S. to try to fix the mess the French had left behind when they lost Indochina. He joined the marines because he thought that if his country was at war he had a duty to serve. Consciously or not, he was emulating my grandfather—his father—also a volunteer who had fought his way across Europe with Patton and twice received the Silver Star in addition to the Distinguished Service Cross and the French Croix de Guerre. The abolition of the draft and the conversion of the U.S. military to an all-volunteer professional force had dismayed my father. So far as he was concerned, the obligation to bear arms and serve was an intrinsic attribute of citizenship, which he thought, surprisingly for a philosopher, must be fulfilled in the spirit of my-country-right-or-wrong.

I asked myself what those brave men—warriors without a trace of bellicosity in them—would think of my saying to myself that this new war is different, that since there is no draft, no legal obligation to serve, it can be left to those who see no great future ahead of themselves, listen to the recruiter's siren song, and enlist, and to the service academy meatheads appointed to lead them. Would they nod approvingly and say that times do change, and while I should, of course, be ready to answer the call to arms if it came, in the meantime my less showy, but just as important, obligation was to honor the terms of my fellowship at Harvard and get on with my research? It was not an unlikely result. My grandfather and father, both of them reasonable men, both opposed to reckless foreign adventures, might well have given me that advice or some near-enough variation on its theme. But I wasn't comfortable with it, and wondered what misgivings they would have felt once they had given it. How likely were they to think that it was small wonder that Harry thought of me as his son.

Harry was out with clients that Saturday evening, but on

Sunday he got home around seven—which for him was on the early side—and announced that after he'd taken his bath and changed he'd cook pasta for our dinner. Spaghetti *aglio e olio*, a garlicky specialty of his laced with crushed red peppers, which I remembered fondly from visits to Sag Harbor. But first we'd have drinks. Over gin martinis, which were another one of his specialties, he told me he'd been meeting with Abner Brown and his second-in-command. The work he was doing for Abner continued to expand in a manner that was flattering to him and was naturally very much appreciated by the firm. The conglomerate of which, except for a small number of joint venture partners, Abner was the sole owner, and also Abner as an individual, had become very important clients. In fact, he worried about the weight of the Brown matters in the firm's business mix, and what he considered the overly optimistic assumptions his partners made concerning its continued growth and even the nature of the relationship itself.

Never rely on the favor of kings or excessively rich men, he said shaking his head. They're heartless and fickle.

In any event, spending more and more time with Abner and being treated by him as an intimate friend, as well as his principal outside counsel, however flattering, was no bed of roses. Harry had made it clear at the outset, when Abner first asked him to represent him and his businesses generally, that while he wasn't active in politics he was a registered Democrat, and the only Republican candidates he'd ever voted for were Nelson Rockefeller and John Lindsay.

As you might expect, he continued, Abner didn't bat an

eye. Considering that he's somewhere to the right of the John Birch Society and Attila the Hun, it isn't just proof of good manners. I think it also means either that he's intelligent enough not to need to surround himself exclusively with fellow true believers—Lord, how I hate that expression!—or, more probably, that he considers the views of someone like me, who doesn't have money to back them up, completely devoid of importance.

Beyond that discomfort, he said, the breadth of Abner's convoluted affairs was such that he feared being swept away in an avalanche of problems without having the time or detachment necessary to grasp the entire background and all the ramifications. He had to beef up his team, but he hadn't figured out yet what mix of skills and personalities he needed. These questions were nagging at his mind, and he was nowhere near a resolution.

Uncle Harry, I broke in, that's a fascinating and difficult situation. I'm really interested, but I have something urgent I must talk to you about. Would you forgive me if I changed the subject?

Of course, he answered, go right ahead.

Over the weekend, I told him, I came to a decision of which I think you'll disapprove. Perhaps you'll think I'm totally fucked up. Here it is. We both see that a war is coming, and I don't think people like me should say, Let's leave the fighting to the other guys, the kids who don't go to Harvard, Yale, or Princeton, or Saint Paul's, the kids who are lucky if they make it through high school, who enlist because other doors are closed and they've been watching fancy television commercials about military training. That's too easy. I want to be in there with them. So unless you talk me out of it I'll do what Dad did: get into the U.S. Marine Officer Candidates School and take it from there.

That's quite a piece of news, he replied. It calls for another batch of martinis. Back in a moment.

It was a suspiciously long moment, lasting five minutes or more, but finally Harry emerged from the pantry with the shaker, refilled my glass and then his, and said very solemnly, Let's drink to your undertaking. You're a nut, but so was your father. And your grandpa. As for me . . . You probably know some version of the story. I was deemed unfit to serve in Vietnam, unfit to cover myself with glory like your father. Well, he got back . . . All I ask is that you don't get yourself killed and do your best to come back in one piece. If possible in better shape than your papa. You're the only person I have left in this world.

Plato, pretending he was a lion, lay in repose on the coffee table, a practice that I had a suspicion Harry didn't just tolerate. He actively encouraged it. Just then the little Burmese raised his head questioningly.

Yes, of course, Harry said, laughing, I have you and thank the Lord I have Plato, who has the good sense not to go off to war. He'll look after his old pal Harry. All joking aside, take good care of yourself and be sure to write a nice letter to the Society of Fellows people. That's a lawyer speaking. You may want to be welcomed back when you return.

II

Nothing mattered to me when I got out of Walter Reed except the desperate, consuming need to get my writing done. I was telling what the fighting had been like, and what it had done to my men and me. I wanted the whole world to know. Had it been possible, I would have shouted the story from rooftops. Harry had said back in 2001 that I was all he had left in this world. Now, seven years later, I could say the same of him: he was my sole remaining link to humanity. Felicity gave up on me quicker than I would have thought possible. She left me while I was patrolling through Musa Qala, and married a fellow archaeologist. I saw it on Facebook. They had a little girl. She sent pictures as though I could give a shit. Later, Facebook told me that she was once again pregnant and hoped for a boy. Did she want to bring up a warrior? My school and college classmates had become lawyers or investment bankers. I had no desire to see any of them. That left Scott Prentice. He had been my classmate at school and we were classmates again at Yale and joined the same college senior society. It didn't take me long to come to the conclusion that he was the smartest man I knew or was likely to know, but so low-key and modest most people didn't have an inkling of the speed with which his mind worked. He was a fine athlete as well, and we were both on the school lacrosse teams. Our school had recruited him as a fencing prodigy, and he stayed with the saber through school and college. Our academic paths diverged at college, and I saw a good deal less of him. Scott had a passion for mathematics. I was wrapped up in my history courses and Greek and Latin classics. In the summers I wangled stints at archaeological sites. We sat next to each other last at a Bones dinner just before graduation and went back to his room afterward to talk. I was disgustingly full of plans for Balliol. Scott confessed he was at loose ends. Graduate school beckoned, perhaps MIT, perhaps Stanford, but he wasn't sure he was ready to commit. His father, a career diplomat and a noted Arabist, at the time serving as the CIA section chief in Beirut, was killed in the bombing of our embassy there in April 1983. Scott and his mother were in New York, on a home visit, when it happened. His mother remarried promptly, and he hardly remembered his father. It was nearly dawn when we drank our last beer, and as we were saying goodbye he told me that he was truly torn. Mathematics was his love. Government service attracted and repelled powerfully. He promised to write and to do his best to visit me in England. In fact, I didn't hear from him, and the letter I sent to the only address I had, his mother's apartment in New York, went unanswered. I thought of calling her, and in the end didn't. She'd been widowed again; I hadn't written to offer my condolences; I felt stupidly embarrassed.

My surprise and delight were extreme when Scott and I ran into each other in Kandahar, shortly before my team moved out to Delaram. He wore an army officer's uniform with a major's golden oak leaf. I'd just made captain. Did that mean that he'd gone to OCS straight out of college, even though we weren't then at war? Even the premonitory attack against the USS *Cole* didn't take place until the fall of 2000. It turned out that that wasn't the reason, but there wasn't time to get into that sort of stuff during the brief cup of coffee at the base PX. I learned that the uniform was a cover, and Scott's real employers were the Special Activities Division boys over at Langley. He told me of his sudden decision to join, and some of the stuff he had been doing, when he came to visit me at Walter Reed, which he did at least once a week. He'd been brought back to headquarters. As we talked about everything we had lived through and the shape of our future, it became clear to me again that he was my closest friend— the brother I had never had. I didn't doubt that was also how he felt about me.

Harry invited me to move in with him as soon as the hospital released me. I accepted without hesitation, because I wanted to be near him and, to tell the truth, in some small part because I had no other place to go. He did everything to make it comfortable for me to work, setting up a large desk, additional bookshelves, and filing cabinets in the guest room that was to be my study. I was to sleep in the smaller guest room. We had dinner together whenever Harry was free, and after a while I realized that he was making an effort to be free most evenings. Dinner was invariably late. That made possible long workdays, without interruptions or respite from my manuscript other than for a sandwich at lunch, runs in the park, and weight lifting and Krav Maga sessions at a Third Avenue gym in which Harry had given me a membership. Push-ups and pull-ups I did at home since Harry, who apparently thought of everything, had had a bar installed in my bathroom. Getting back as near as humanly possible into Force Recon shape had become, next to the book, an obsession. My other daytime forays from the apartment were few and far between. I would slink back to the apartment revolted by the luxury of store-window displays and the parading princesses of Madison Avenue—skinny tall girls with big hair, big tits, big sunglasses, and big shoulder bags talking into their big phones—and sickened by pity, pity like a newborn babe striding the blast, for soldiers still stuck in the hellholes I'd known, for veterans coming home to a country that didn't give a shit, for everyone who'd been dealt a lousy hand. Even for myself, although I knew that my case was different, that eventually I would recover and never face the indignities and desperations the others would.

I gave Harry the complete draft of my book on a Friday so rainy that he'd decided not to go out to Sag Harbor. This is very exciting, he said, and started reading right after dinner. He kept at it the entire weekend, practically nonstop. He read in his library, the door to which was always open. Unable to restrain myself, I found reasons to pass by from time to time and check whether he was still at it. I think he was too absorbed to notice. We had dinner together on Saturday, but neither of us said a word that touched on the book. I thought Harry was filibustering, talking endlessly about Abner Brown and his new investments in Peru, Argentina, Chile, and Pakistan because I had disappointed him and he hadn't figured out how to break that to me. By the time we'd eaten our dessert I was falling asleep at the table. On Sunday afternoon I was in despair and went to the gym for a long workout. When I returned I found a note on the table in the foyer asking me to stop by the library.

I've finished your book, he said. Some parts I've read more than twice. I wish your parents were alive. They'd be very proud of you, but no prouder than I.

I knew no one in literary New York, no writers, no agents, and no editors. Harry steered me to Jane Bird, a young agent who took me on as a client and has become a friend. Harry had obtained an introduction to her through a cultural reporter at the *Times* married to a partner in his firm. The first publisher to whom Jane offered the book bought it and decided to publish on an accelerated six-month schedule, in October. A few weeks later Jane succeeded in selling a film option to a studio on terms so favorable that they staggered me. Astonishingly, incredibly, I was launched. When I tried to thank him, Harry just laughed and laughed. He came up with the line that whatever he was doing for me and my book was done for the honor of the family. In a more serious mode, he told me that he'd give a big party in October to celebrate me and the book. It's time you met some people who count, he said. He also talked about the summer. He intended to be in Sag Harbor on weekends as often as possible—It's good for my pal Plato, he claimed—and to take all of August there, returning to the city only after Labor Day. He hoped I would join him in Sag Harbor often—as often as the spirit moved me. But I didn't go out in August at all. Work on galleys and related chores were easier to handle if I was in New York, and I had started work on my second book and felt a powerful need to be alone. All the same, when Harry invited me specifically for the Labor Day weekend, I accepted. The work on the new book was progressing; the chores relating to what I now called the old book were done; I felt I could use a couple of good swims in the ocean.

Harry said he was delighted. There are people in the Hamptons you ought to know, he told me. A number of them will be at your book party. The Labor Day party will be a rehearsal for the real McCoy in October.

I got to Sag Harbor that weekend on Friday morning. The house was as beautiful as I remembered it, and in spectacularly good order. That is Mary's doing, Harry told me, and, introducing me to a small and pretty young woman, explained that she had immigrated from Ireland, married, and divided her time between her and her husband's pet shop on Route 27 in Wainscott and what she called the care and grooming of Harry.

And watching your uncle Harry play with Plato, she chimed in. Those two are really something.

We had a quick sandwich in the garden and drove to Gibson Lane, the Sagaponack ocean beach that was Harry's favorite. It too was unchanged, splendidly white and endless under a sky of unbearably intense blue. Even though it was the beginning of the busiest weekend of the summer, and the weather was glorious, we didn't need to walk more than a hundred yards east from the entrance where Harry had parked to be completely alone. Harry put down our beach bag, and we took off our shirts and ran into the waves. He was a great swimmer, and it was he who taught me, when I first started to visit him, to play safely with giant breakers. The key, he had told me over and over, is to be watchful but relaxed, watchful but relaxed. They're not out to get you. It's just that they're infinitely stronger. You have to outsmart them or go with the flow. We bodysurfed together that afternoon and each of the following three days. Then I swam alone eastward as far as Peter's Pond Beach and back. That was a swim that Harry and I used to do together. This time he demurred. I get winded, he said. Otherwise, he was in good shape, and in excellent spirits. I was to go right ahead and take as much time as I liked. He didn't mind waiting. Or he might walk along the shore in my direction, so as not to miss me.

When we got back to the house Harry said that he'd made no plans to go out on Saturday or Sunday or to have people over. He was tired of the Hampton weekend madness and looked forward to trying out his new pasta recipes. That was just fine with me. I was finding it hard to keep the new book out of my thoughts and welcomed being able to devote to it and to playing with Plato the hours we did not spend at the beach or at table. In order to be able to let Plato out without worrying that he'd dash into the street and get hit by a car, Harry had the entire plot in back of the house—lawn and garden—surrounded by a six-foot stockade fence that not even the most enterprising Burmese tomcat could dream of scaling, and no marauding deer could jump. There was only one opening in it, a door leading to the adjoining garden. Harry explained that way back in the nineteenth century that garden and the house to which it belonged, as well as his house, had been the property of two sisters, and tradition required that the entrance be maintained.

It's fine with me, he said. The other house belongs to my dear friend, the wonderful Sasha Evans, and as you see we've made the door Plato-proof. He only goes to Sasha's garden when he's invited.

Until then I had taken with a grain of salt Harry's claims that his Fifth Avenue kitty would arrive in Sag Harbor, have a snack of dry food and a drink of water, and, so refreshed, roll up his sleeves and start killing. Now I saw that he hadn't been exaggerating. There were no mice left on the property, but it was still home to a population of chipmunks. Plato outthought and outran them, an achievement that had consistently eluded my parents' cats, themselves no slouches. In spite of Harry's declared intention, we did have a dinner guest on Sunday, that same Sasha, Harry's next-door neighbor. She's a fine landscape painter, Harry explained before she arrived, born and bred in Boston, widowed some years back, with one daughter living in Oregon. She'd called to invite him to dinner that evening at the last minute, explaining she was alone and blue. Naturally he'd yielded to his better nature and asked her to dine instead with us at his house. They're made for each other, I kept saying to myself while we were having a drink, after I'd taken a good look at her and listened to their conversation, and later over Harry's gnocchi. They're the same sort of people; she's his age; they could have a good life. Why doesn't he go for it? I could think of one reason only. If the element of strong sexual attraction was missing—I couldn't detect even a whiff of any such thing—would Harry or she risk having a marriage or a liaison go sour? Or even risk an exploratory gesture, with the potential for embarrassment and disappointment it entailed? I didn't think it likely. They preferred to leave things as they were, to be the best of neighbors and friends, and would recoil from anything that might put that easy and comforting relationship in peril.

The Labor Day weekend weather continued to be superb, with sunny skies and low humidity, and the mini–book party took place on the lawn behind Harry's house. I had always thought of Sag Harbor as the Hampton haunt of Upper West Side writers, editors, literary agents, and journalists accoutered in all seasons in L.L. Bean camp gear. In fact a great many of them gathered at the party, as did an even larger population of elderly quintessential WASPs, who I supposed—wrongly, as it turned out—were all investment bankers and their second or third wives, spectrally thin women arrayed in white, yellow, and lime silk and once-husky and now frail men in white linen and cotton, whom Harry must have drawn from precincts of Sag Harbor I hadn't previously explored or from East Hampton, Bridgehampton, and Southampton. The two populations mingled noisily and in great harmony. I remained at Harry's side, as he had instructed me, until the garden was filled to overflowing, and Harry said it was time to circulate. I took that as permission to make a beeline for

Sasha. She led me by the hand to a pair of unoccupied chairs, and we remained there until Harry, smiling from ear to ear, came to take me to task for monopolizing the most irresistible woman at the party and to say that in half an hour we three would be having dinner at the American Hotel. He had hoped that Kerry Black, an associate working for him, would join us and balance the table, but she'd called earlier to report she was stuck in the office, trying to meet a deadline. It's really too bad, he said, particularly since the deadline is one that I imposed!

The official party Harry gave for my book took place at his club on the publication date, which was Wednesday in the second week of October. The only personal guests invited by me—real people, is how I described them to Harry—were Scott Prentice and my Third Avenue gym trainer, Wolf. My agent, Jane, and my editor had suggested to Harry the professional types to put on his list. They were so numerous, and so expertly chosen, that after I had shaken their hands I could truthfully claim that out of the class of New Yorkers who could be normally found at a fancy literary party, complete with French champagne and the best hors d'oeuvres, there was not one I had not met. The others were, of course, Harry's old friends, some of them from his firm, Simon Lathrop and his wife among them. I want to show you off, he had told me, as though you were my son. Indeed, talking to some of those grand lawyers and their wives, I discovered that they knew a great deal about my exploits at Yale and in the Corps. My uncle Harry had been boasting about me!

Among the handful of younger J & W lawyers I was immediately drawn to an athletically built girl almost as tall as I with a delicate pale face, eyes that were more green than blue, and a huge chignon of curly black hair. She turned out to be Harry's protégée, Kerry. I told her how sorry Harry had been when she had to miss the Labor Day invitation in Sag Harbor, and how eager he had made me to meet her.

I've been pretty eager to meet you as well! she replied. Most of my conversations with Harry are about client stuff and all the things he wants to get done or redone before the end of the day. But, if there is ever a pause, he talks about you.

That must be a real bore, I said.

She shook her head so vigorously that her chignon was in danger of coming undone. She raised her hands to fix it, giving me an opportunity to admire her toned and sexy arms.

No, she said, it makes me happy because recounting your adventures and accomplishments has the best effect on him. You may not realize it, but he's under a lot of pressure and works too hard. It's a real tonic for him to know that you're out of danger and that you've written a book that he thinks is so good and so genuine.

I think you like him, I said.

That's an understatement!

With that she shook my hand and said she was going back to work—guess for whom!

I told Harry about my brief chat with Kerry and that I wished she hadn't hurried back to the office. He nodded and said there was no one like her—she was, quite simply, the brightest and most conscientious associate he had ever worked with. She'd be up for partnership soon, perhaps the following year, and he intended to put his heart and soul into making sure she was taken in. A most unusual case, he added, a first-class litigator who cuts through the most devilishly intricate corporate structures and, on top of that, has innate business sense. She knows what's important! She came to us fresh from law school—Harvard, as a matter of fact—then put in three years prosecuting white-collar criminals of all stripes as an assistant U.S. attorney in the Southern District, and, fortunately, returned to us.

Are you now also doing litigation for Abner? I asked.

The firm is, he replied. I don't handle it personally, but I'm in overall charge of everything we do for them, and having her at my side on litigations as well as on corporate work is a godsend. You could say she's my chief of staff.

There seemed no end to the care Harry took of me. I had said, about the time Jane sold the film option on my book, that much as I loved living with him I should probably try to become a real grown-up and get a place of my own. Far from protesting, he told me I was right. As it happened, the daughter of one of his partners was a crackerjack real estate agent. He thought I should put myself in her hands. I took his advice, and very quickly she found a small apartment just off Park Avenue, a few blocks north of Harry, with exactly the space and layout I needed. Harry's one complaint was that the building had no doorman. Just two locked doors at each of which you had to ring and wait to be buzzed in.

Not a good idea, he said. The city isn't dangerous now, but you don't want to have to worry about that sort of thing, or about deliveries. Especially if you travel.

Harry, I replied, I'm a trained killer! No mugger's going to mess with me or my .45.

The little apartment was absurdly expensive; that was my only complaint, I told Harry and asked whether I should really spend all that money.

Look, Jack, he said, this is the Upper East Side. Prices are crazy. But you're a rich man now, and the way things are going you'll only get richer.

I stopped arguing. The film of the first book was already in production, and I'd gotten paid for the rights. Coming on top of the option money, it put me in possession of more money than I had ever dreamed of having.

I saw less of Harry over the next year and a half or so while I was finishing the new book, revising it, and seeing it through the editing process. We did have dinner at least once a week, and sometimes, if he spent the weekend in the city, we went to the movies together. On a few weekends I joined him in Sag Harbor. There was another source, in addition to my work, of demands on my time. I had made a play for an unattached young Englishwoman working at my publisher's. In and out of bed, she reminded me of Felicity. It was the way she talked and dressed and, to tell the truth, her scant regard for certain aspects of personal hygiene. I liked her well enough to introduce her to a somewhat-skeptical Harry but not to have her move in with me. Our initial arrangement, dinner at one greasy spoon or another followed by a sleepover at my apartment, suited me just fine. I could tell that she'd interfere with my work, and that, if our romance soured, she'd be difficult to evict. The more sensible course was for her to hang on to her share of the East Village apartment convenient by subway to the publishing house, which was near Union Square, and to the Eighty-Sixth Street stop of the Number 4 or Number 6 train. She took that badly, apparently unable to understand my need to safeguard my working space and my new book. We broke off, without undue acrimony, shortly before I handed in the manuscript.

Once again, I showed my book to Harry, even more nervous than about my first because, being a story with echoes of my years at prep school and Yale, it inevitably included allusions to my parents that he could not fail to recognize. And once again, he delighted me by reading with all the sympathy I might have wished for. My publisher was pleased too and, repeating the pattern established with the first book, decided to rush into print. This time the book party was given by the publishing house, a fact that in this day of shrinking promotion budgets for anything but soft-porn blockbusters could be taken as a feather in my cap. The gathered literati were even grander than at my first party, but very few of Harry's law firm colleagues were in attendance. Perhaps my publisher had suggested that Harry prune that part of the list. Kerry Black, of course, was there, as well as Scott Prentice and my trainer, Wolf. Harry had understood that my publisher's giving the party signaled the commitment of the house to my book and, as he put it, had resigned himself to not being the host. He insisted, however, on his right to give a small dinner afterward. The guests, in addition to my editor, were my agent, Harry's country neighbor the beautiful

Sasha, and, of course, Scott and Kerry. Kerry had become a partner, an event that I had been invited to help celebrate at a dinner also given by Harry. After dinner, I took Kerry home.

She lived on Fifty-Seventh Street, in the last block before the East River. As I hoped, she asked me to come up and have a drink in her apartment. It amused me to see that it was very much like mine: the same security system judged so irritatingly inadequate by Harry, painfully neat—presumably a permanent condition since she had no reason to expect a visitor—and full of books. I told her that I had agreed to do a few readings and interviews spread over the next couple of weeks and that, once those obligations were discharged, I was going to travel in South America, part of the time with Scott, whom she had just met. If possible we'd get as far as the end of Tierra del Fuego, mostly hiking and cycling. Scott was sorting out the details.

That's the trip of my dreams, she said.

Come with us, I told her. We'd love it, and we're both pretty good at camping. You won't have to lift a finger.

I'd come in a heartbeat, was her answer, but there are two problems: Harry, who needs me at his side, and work for him that has to be done. There isn't a chance of my going on vacation before next summer, and even then I doubt I'll be able to take more than a week or two at a time.

Then she asked me how long I'd be in South America.

Three months, I told her, give or take a week.

I see, she said. Harry will be very glad when you return. Please don't take what I say amiss, but you and Plato—she laughed—yes, Plato too, are very good at taking the weight off his shoulders or heart or wherever it lies, so I hope that between these speaking engagements you'll find some time for him. It would make him so happy!

I thanked her and made two resolutions. The first was to be with Harry as much as possible before I left for Belize, which was to be my first stop. The second was to see a great deal of Kerry when I returned.

I kept the first resolution, as well as, in circumstances I could not then foresee, the second.

III

Our exploration of Tierra del Fuego over, Scott and I caught a TAM flight to São Paulo at the Ushuaia Airport. From there he went on to D.C., and I flew to Cuiabá. I was met at its airport by an employee of Pedra Negra, a huge cattle ranch deep in the Mato Grosso savanna, who drove me to the fazenda in an immaculately clean white Range Rover. Pedra Negra's absentee owner, Dirk van der Sluyten, a Dutch industrialist client and friend of Harry's, had bought it in the 1980s, with Harry's assistance, in consequence of an imbroglio that Harry said was melodramatic, from the patriarch of an old Brazilian Carioca family that owned half of downtown Rio de Janeiro. The Dutchman had been begging Harry ever since—unsuccessfully—to stay at the fazenda, which he had visited only once, overnight, before the closing, and use it as if it were his own. Harry had never gotten around to it, but, when I told him that Scott would have to rush back to D.C., and I would be wandering around alone in Brazil, he remembered the invitation.

Go to Pedra Negra instead, he told me. It's like no place you've ever seen and no place you'll ever see. You've been saying you want to put in a few weeks working hard on your book. Do it there. It's the ideal place. So far as the climate is concerned, this is the best time of the year. Hot, but you won't mind that. There will be no distractions and no temptations. Who knows? If everything breaks right, perhaps I'll come out and join you, and Lord knows I've never interfered with your writing.

I said it was a great idea and I would think about it. But Harry didn't wait for my decision. He wrote to his friend about me, and two days later a letter arrived addressed to me, expressing delight at my forthcoming arrival and enclosing photographs of a vast brown wooden structure, which was the fazenda's main house, as well as an introduction to Alberto Ferreira, the ranch manager. My hand had been forced. I sent an email to Mr. van der Sluyten gratefully accepting his invitation. The next day I had lunch with Harry. When I told him what I had done, he said he was delighted, and it wasn't until the end of the meal that he told me he had a disclosure to make. There were complications in his dealings with Abner Brown that made it absolutely impossible for him even to think of a vacation, however brief, anytime soon. He hoped his absence would contribute to my productivity.

Alberto, who was waiting for me at the main house when I arrived, and apologized time and time again for not having come to the airport, showed me around. I was to be the sole inhabitant. Dona Marisa, the woman who would cook my meals, and her husband, Seu Wellington, a gardener doubling as a houseman, lived in a small structure down the road. They had a working landline telephone connection, and there was one in the main house as well, a necessity, Alberto explained, if I wanted to reach them or him, there being no cell-phone reception in this part of Pedra Negra. Likewise, there was no Internet connection either at the main house or at his, Alberto's, office or house. One of Mr. van der Sluyten's peeves was having to communicate with him by fax instead of email. Was that going to be a problem for me? Alberto asked. If it was he could look into the availability of a dial-up connection. I laughed and said that if it had been possible to get online in the house I would have disabled that function on my laptop. When I congratulated him on his English, which was completely fluent though occasionally embellished by unusual locutions, he told me that he had attended Purdue University's school of agriculture.

Pedra Negra is a very serious cattle ranch, he assured me. We treat our herd on the highest professional level.

He also told me that I shouldn't be surprised by the level of security at the ranch. A detail on horseback patrolled the area around the main house from dusk to dawn, and there were motorized patrols at the ranch's perimeter. There are very many bad people in the Mato Grosso, Captain Jack, he said, and asked whether I would like him to lend me a weapon for the duration of my stay, one I could keep in my bedroom. I told him to stop calling me captain, and that I'd be grateful for the loan of a weapon. Later, Wellington placed a huge Smith & Wesson .357 Magnum on my night table and a box of ammunition on the floor. If you want to try it, Alberto said, there is a range complete with targets just beyond the swimming pool that Wellington can show you. Dr. Dirk—that was how he referred to his employer—enjoys pistol and rifle target practice.

Once more Harry had proved to be the most efficient and best of uncles. If a writer truly wanted solitude, the fazenda was a dream house. I wasted no time getting to work, and soon settled into an ideal routine: a three-to-five-mile run in the very early morning during which I was often followed at a distance by the horseback patrol, breakfast served on the open veranda by Dona Marisa, three hours of work, forty-five minutes of laps in the pool, lunch consisting of cold meat or eggs and crème de papaya—which I loved—or fruit for dessert, a nap, another three or four hours of work, target practice, a second more-relaxed swim, and finally dinner, with Catupiry, a soft and very mild white cheese, accompanied by guava jelly to round out the meal. I went to bed early, after deciphering, with the help of my Latin, French, and rudimentary Spanish, my sole source of news, the Portuguese-language *Estado do São Paulo* deposited on the veranda by Seu Wellington. That was how I learned, among other horrors of the day that crowded its pages, of the stampede at the Port Said stadium, where seventy-nine were killed and thousands injured after a match, a monstrosity that struck so resonant a chord even in soccer-crazy Brazil that Alberto drove over to the main house to discuss it and the differences in national character that in his opinion accounted for the outrages committed by fans. Afterward, he asked to join me on the range. Wellington had been telling him about my prowess, and he had brought his own pistol, a 9mm Beretta. We banged away companion-ably, and as he was a good shot I was glad to outscore him. When he congratulated me, I made no attempt to hide my satisfaction, saying that the Smith & Wesson had taken some getting used to—my own sidearm being a modified Colt MI911 .45 ACP, which I was sorry to say I hadn't fired once since I became a civilian. I was grateful to him for getting me back into form. That was the truth. I had gotten the idea that even though I was a full-time scribbler I should keep in shape and continue to hone personal combat skills, or come as close as was feasible without being back on active duty.

As the end of the third week of my stay approached, I allowed myself a peek at the word count on my computer and saw that I had written just about a fourth of my novel as I then conceived it. That called for a celebration, and I accepted with alacrity and genuine pleasure two invitations Alberto extended. The first was to take an abbreviated tour of the ranch, from which I had previously begged off. I would at last meet his cows! The second was to a churrasco at his house. He wanted me to taste some of those very cows' colleagues, as well as other barbecue delicacies.

The cattle—some thousand head, according to Alberto—waited for us when we arrived in their proximity after half an hour's drive across the strangely exhilarating empty vastness of the savanna. Lined up in rows, perhaps thirty abreast, like infantry of a bygone era on parade, and flanked by cowboys instead of drill sergeants, the steers were spectrally white, built low to the ground, and somber looking, with promi-nent humps on their backs. Alberto explained that they were

Brahman cattle, originating in India, bred for meat, polled to avoid injury in case of arguments. They were the prevalent breed in Brazil, especially in the Mato Grosso, for the same reason they were widely appreciated in India: their ability to thrive in very hot weather.

We have some milk cows on the fazenda, he added, just enough to make our own butter and Catupiry, but that's only a hobby. The name of the game is meat—better meat than in Argentina. You will see when we get together tonight.

He was right. I had never eaten better steak. We drank caipirinhas, delectable concoctions combining cachaça, a powerful liquor made from fresh sugarcane juice, lime, and sugar—he advised me to have them prepared with only a pinch of sugar—and then beer, which is what everyone at the party seemed to be drinking, although Alberto showed me the two bottles of a very respectable Pauillac he had withdrawn in my honor from Dr. Dirk's cellar upon the boss's express orders. Alberto being the only real English speaker in this group of ranch supervisors and their knockout wives, all of whom, Alberto's wife, Sonia, included, having quickly given up the effort to entertain me by their conversation, we sat down together in a pair of comfortable armchairs on the veranda and talked. It was thus that I heard, in addition to endless statistics about the productivity of Pedra Negra, an account of the circumstances that had led old Dr. Sampaio to sell to Mynheer van der Sluyten the fazenda that had been in the Sampaio family for generations. It was nothing less than the failure to take revenge as required by the Mato Grosso code of honor, and the disgrace and ostracism that followed.

You understand, Jack, Alberto said, there aren't very many people in the Mato Grosso, and some are very bad. I've told you that. It's the reason we pay so much attention to security. So when the eldest of the Santos brothers gunned down Ricardo, Dr. Sampaio's ranch manager—the man who had my job—in cold blood, at the front door of this very house, with Ricardo's wife and children watching from inside, got back into his truck, and drove away, there was only one honorable course for the old man to follow. The Santos are real thugs and run a vicious protection racket. No one expected Dr. Sampaio to kill José Santos himself: he was too old, and it wasn't a job for someone like him anyway. But considering that the reason Ricardo was killed was that he wouldn't pay protection money to the Santos gang and wouldn't let them rustle Pedra Negra cattle, Dr. Sampaio had a duty to find someone who would do the job. Hire a professional. Well, the old gentleman said, those days were gone. He would go to the police. Everybody knew that was a big joke, because no policeman, no prosecutor, no judge in Mato Grosso would touch a hair on the head of a Santos. They all want to live, and they want their wives and children to live, and just between you and me they like the little presents they receive from the Santos. I don't need to tell you, Jack, that government officials in Brazil aren't paid a decent salary. So in short order it became impossible for Dr. Sampaio to come to the ranch. The personnel wouldn't look at him, the cattle were falling sick, everything was going wrong. Finally, he got the point and announced that he would sell the ranch. And that's where Dr. Dirk came in, and that's where I came in too.

You? I asked, genuinely surprised.

Yes, Dr. Dirk hired me because of my credentials in cattle-ranch management and also because I'm a local—my family has been here forever—and he thought I'd know what needed to be done. I sure did. I wasn't going to waste my time going to the authorities, and I wasn't going to the bars in Cuiabá to hire a hit man. You never know if one of those guys is going to work for you or for the opposition, particularly if the opposition is the Santos, or when and how he's going to shake you down after the job is done. On the other hand, I didn't want to go to jail for the rest of my life for murder after I'd wasted José Santos. Dr. Dirk wasn't going to protect me from the authorities. He wouldn't know how, and anyway didn't have that kind of pull. No foreigner does in the Mato Grosso. What do you think was the solution? Simple! I had to kill the bastard in self-defense. So I put the word out that I was going to get José, in order to square the accounts at Pedra Negra, and that for a week I'd be waiting for him at nightfall on the porch outside my office. If he still had real balls on him, I'd say to whoever would listen, and let me tell you a lot of people didn't dare to listen, he can come on a visit. So the week I named came, and I sat there on the porch in a nice armchair just like this one with my nice twelve-gauge Remington shotgun in my lap, bottle of cachaça at my side, waiting. Waiting. I start on Monday. Waiting patiently. Tuesday night I put the record player on in my office and open the window to be able to hear the music better. *Cha-cha-cha!* Thank God, we have no mosquitoes in this part of the ranch. Nothing on Monday, nothing on Tuesday. On Wednesday *baaaam!* José pulls up in his truck, gets out, waves hello. I see that in his left hand he's got a fifty-caliber Smith & Wesson—I didn't know the son of a bitch was a lefty—and I think he's going to let me have it. But no! He laughs like a fucking hyena. In his right hand he holds a grenade, pulls the pin with his teeth, and *whoosh* tosses it on the porch. Only then he empties his magazine. You can't imagine the racket—or maybe you can, if you think of Iraq or Afghanistan. That's the end of me, right? Wrong! Because it wasn't me in the armchair on the porch. I'd put a dummy, dressed and made up to look like me. He must have been mainlining stuff not to realize something was wrong, that the guy in the armchair wasn't reacting to anything. Just keeping a stiff upper lip! Ha! Ha! Ha! The real me had always been holed up in a nice reinforced blind I'd built for myself under the porch. His hand grenade—no sweat! From there, my other Remington nicely braced, I emptied it right into José's face. After I'd finished, he had no head left.

Holy cow, I said. So then you called the police, right?

Alberto nodded.

And you were in the clear?

Right again.

And how come the other Santos brothers haven't come to get you?

Because it was a vengeance killing. He'd killed Ricardo, and I made him pay for it. The accounts were settled. That's the Mato Grosso way. Once we're even, we don't keep going.

The next morning, he drove me to the airport. I promised to come back, and he promised to visit me in New York. He'd bring Sonia. She told him after the party that she'd get to work on her English.

· · ·

The plane for Brasília, where I was going to get on a Varig flight to New York, was late. I didn't mind. The waiting lounge at the Cuiabá airport was clean, and there was a functioning Wi-Fi connection. What's more, the layover in Brasília was long. According to the functionary at the information desk, there was no risk of missing my connection. With something akin to resignation, I turned on my laptop and logged on to Gmail. It was as I had feared: a seemingly endless queue of messages. I rearranged them so that the oldest would be on top and found, practically adjacent to each other, two emails. One was from Kerry, dated January 9. The subject line read: Harry. Extremely Urgent. The message was brief: Harry died yesterday. Please call me as soon as you can at one of the following numbers. I recognized her home number. The other was a cell-phone number, which was not her office BlackBerry. I was struck by that, and by the fact that she did not ask me to call her at the office, but didn't know what to make of it. The second, sent two days later, was from Fred Minot. Like Kerry's, it had been sent from Jones & Whetstone, Harry's law firm. I knew Minot's name. He was the J & W trusts and estates lawyer whom Harry had gotten to do my will. It's absurd, he'd said, that I should inherit if something happened to you. You should leave your money to Yale or some cultural institutions. This too was a brief message: I'm the preliminary executor under the will of Harry Dana who has passed away. Please contact me at your early convenience.

I got a cup of coffee. Realizing that my hands were trembling, I made an effort to control the tremor and called

Kerry's cell-phone number. It was early afternoon in New York. There was no reason that she should be at home. She answered at once and asked that I call the same number again in fifteen minutes. That is what I did, and once again she answered at the first ring.

It's so awful, Jack, she said. He killed himself. He hanged himself, in Sag Harbor, in that beautiful studio in back of his house. From one of those beams he was so proud of.

Why, why? I asked her. Did something happen? Did he find out he was sick, some particularly awful sort of cancer?

I asked that question because Harry had told me more than once, beginning with the time when my father went into a coma after the stroke, that he was determined to avoid being kept alive if he came down with an incurable disease. At the time he was a member of the Hemlock Society—I didn't know whether that organization still existed—and I knew that he had made preparations for the eventuality of having to take his leave, which was how he referred to killing himself. He hoarded sleeping pills and owned both a straight razor and a surgical lancet, being of the opinion that opening one's veins was on balance the surest and least painful method. A crisscross cut, he said, was the best, because it's the hardest for some medical interloper to repair. I'd never heard him mention hanging himself as a form of suicide he'd choose. And why hadn't he waited until I returned, so that we could say goodbye? Unless—the thought flashed through my mind—he had concluded that doing it while I was away would spare me.

Did he have cancer? I asked once again.

No, she answered, I know for a fact he was in excellent health. He'd been to see his doctor in the week before Christmas and he said the doctor was happy about his bloods, his numbers, all that stuff. There was absolutely nothing wrong with him.

Was there a letter for me, some other form of explanation?

No, Jack, she said, absolutely nothing, no letter was found.

So why, why, why? I wailed.

I don't know, Jack, she replied. All I can say is that he had been under pressure related to work and had experienced some recent unpleasantness. He decided rather suddenly to retire. I will tell you about it when we see each other.

Your email is from four weeks ago. Is that when it happened? I asked stupidly.

Four weeks ago last Sunday, she answered.

And no one tried to reach me!

Jack, I did try to reach you, I sent you that urgent email. I tried to call you on your cell phone. I had no other way to find you.

What about Harry's secretary? She could've gotten hold of the owner of the ranch where I was staying. He would have called the manager or given her the number.

Jack, she said again, don't you know—no, of course you don't, Barbara Diamond is dead too. I know this is going to be hard to believe, but there was an awful accident. We can talk more about it when I see you, but she was killed the next day by a subway train.

There was a silence. What else was there to say? My uncle and his longtime secretary had both died within a day of each other while I was blissfully drinking caipirinhas. I was having trouble aborting my new reality.

She broke the silence, asking, When will you be back in the city?

I told her my plane was due to land the next morning, early.

There is a great deal we need to talk about, she said. Can you meet me for lunch at Osaka?

That was a restaurant near her office. I replied that I'd be there at whatever hour suited her.

Then come at twelve-thirty, she said.

Before hanging up, I mentioned the email from Minot and asked what she thought I should do about it.

Call him, she told me. You can see him after lunch. But I'd rather you didn't tell him that you and I are getting together first. In fact, please don't tell him we've spoken.

I didn't ask her the reason. I dialed Minot's number and was put through to him right away.

He wasted no time on condolences or small talk of any other kind. Mr. Dana, he said, your uncle Harry Dana committed suicide about four weeks ago. To be precise, he hanged himself at his home in Sag Harbor. Since we were unable to reach you we took the necessary steps. He was cremated. His ashes await your decision as to their disposal. There was a funeral service, of course, at the Christ Episcopal Church out there. As you may know, I'm the executor under your uncle's last will and testament. That means I settle his affairs and distribute his assets after provision for expenses and taxes. As you may also know, apart from some minor bequests, including one to that church, he has left everything to you.

It's a substantial estate. You and I should meet to discuss the implications.

I found the way he'd spoken oddly formal and unpleasant. Not more than two years had gone by since he drew my will and supervised my signing it. We had a sandwich afterward in the firm's cafeteria. Had he forgotten that he called me Jack? Was my memory failing me as well? I recalled Harry's telling me some months ago that he had signed a codicil to his testament naming me executor in the place of Minot. Would Harry have changed his mind again? I decided against raising that question and, instead, thanked Minot and told him that I was on my way back to the U.S. I could be at his office tomorrow between two-thirty and three.

There was a delay during which he seemed to be consulting his secretary. That would be fine, he said in the end, my schedule is clear. Building security will know about your visit and will direct you to the floor on which I'll meet you.

With that he hung up.

IV

The housekeeper found him, Kerry said, that nice Irish girl.

Mary, I murmured. The young woman who also runs a pet shop.

Kerry nodded.

She came to work on Monday morning as usual, at ten, expecting that Harry would have left by then for the city in accordance with established routine, and was surprised to see his Audi still in the garage. The front door was locked, which was strange because Harry always left it on the latch when he was at home. But she needed to open only the doorknob lock. Not the dead bolt, which he would have locked if he had gone away. Anyway, she opened the door using her own key, went into the house, and shouted loudly: Hello, Harry, this is Mary, I'm here! There was no reply. But she began to worry when she went into the kitchen and saw no trace anywhere of dinner or breakfast dishes. He certainly wouldn't have washed and put away breakfast dishes. Had he had an accident? And where was Plato? The cat hadn't come out to greet her. You know how that cat is, she said. He knows exactly where you are, and it had never happened before that Plato had ignored her. He was her friend. So she raced through the house looking for Harry and the cat. Harry's bed hadn't been slept in. The cat wasn't in any of his usual sleeping places. If Harry had gotten a ride into the city and taken Plato, or for some crazy reason had taken the Jitney, wouldn't he have left a note for her? Her heart, she said, began to beat so loud and so fast she thought her chest would burst. She hadn't yet checked the studio, and she rushed there. And that's where she found Harry hanging from a rope attached to one of the high barn beams, face green, tongue sticking out, eyes bulging—and on the ground, right by the desk, lay Plato. His neck had been wrung. Harry must have done it!

Tears were streaming down Kerry's face. I put my hand over hers and told her that this part of the story was impossible, plain wrong. Harry would have never hurt his cat. It can't be. He'd have rather died.

That's what I thought, said Kerry, and that is what I told Mary, but she just repeated the description of what she had seen. I think she's an intelligent and levelheaded woman, but she was in shock.

She wiped the tears streaming down her face.

I asked what happened next.

She called the police, Kerry said, and then she called poor Barbara Diamond—you know, Harry's secretary. Harry had her name and telephone numbers, at home and at the office, up on the bulletin board in the kitchen as the person to get in touch with if there was an urgent problem, an emergency. Barbara didn't answer, but the receptionist picked up, and as soon as she grasped what Mary was calling about she transferred her to Will Hobson, the chairman of the firm. She called me next, and I called Will to ask whether I could help. But he was already on the phone with the police, and he left for Hauppauge to identify Harry at the morgue without calling me back. The Suffolk County medical examiner is in Hauppauge. That's why he went there, and that's where they performed the autopsy.

I guess I looked puzzled because she added, This is standard procedure in cases of suicide as well as suspected violence.

Did the autopsy show anything beyond the obvious?

No. Will got the report a week or ten days ago and showed it to me. I was surprised he did. I'm not in his good graces. It was straightforward. Cause of death: consistent with hanging. No signs of struggle or other observable trauma. The amount of alcohol in the body was consistent with Harry's having had one or two glasses of wine at lunch. Death was estimated to have occurred between seven and nine in the evening, on Sunday. So he could have been hanging for more than twelve hours!

And no letter for me? I'd asked her that on the telephone, but I still couldn't believe it.

No, Jack, nothing. Nothing has been found.

And what have they done with his body? Fred Minot told me over the telephone when I called him yesterday that there had been a service at a church in Sag Harbor.

She began to cry again, and once again I tried to comfort her. Finally she said, Will Hobson or the T & E partner, Minot, arranged for Harry to be cremated. One or the other of them has told me that the funeral parlor in Sag Harbor is holding the ashes for you. And yes, there was a service in Sag Harbor and, of course, I attended. Who else came from the firm? Let's see, Will Hobson and Minot, and I'm pretty sure all the associates who'd worked for Harry. Most of the partners of Harry's vintage and a few who have retired recently. The firm arranged transportation to Sag Harbor and back. Will spoke, quite briefly, and then that nice painter neighbor of Harry's, Sasha Evans, made a beautiful speech. Exactly the eulogy Harry would have wanted. The sermon was good too. You could tell that the priest really knew Harry and wasn't dishing out the usual canned bullshit. Here, she added. I clipped for you the firm's paid announcement of Harry's death that ran in the *Times*.

It gave the date of death, which was an apparent suicide at Harry's Sag Harbor home, his graduation summa cum laude and magna cum laude from Harvard College and Harvard Law School, the clerkships on the Court of Appeals for the Second Circuit and the Supreme Court, the years spent as an associate and a leading partner at J&W, and the date and place of the funeral service.

Rather dry, I said. Is that how these things are usually written? I take it there was no real obituary.

She shook her head. They've become exceedingly rare in the case of someone like Harry, who wasn't in any way a public figure. You'd have to know someone high up in the *Times* hierarchy and get whoever it is to pull strings. But you're right about the paid notice. It's really standoffish. But it's possible they just didn't know how to handle a suicide.

And Plato? Has he been cremated as well?

Kerry shook her head and admitted she didn't know. Then she added, I bet that's something that Mary took care of.

Mary and the phone call to Barbara—my God, I must be losing my mind! What about Barbara? You told me when I called from Cuiabá that she was dead, that there had been a subway accident. I was in such a state of shock that I didn't think to ask you exactly what had happened.

I must be losing my mind too, she said, I keep forgetting that you don't know. It was a ghastly accident, plastered for days on the front pages of the *Post* and *Daily News*. It even made the *Times*. As I told you, Mary found Harry's body on Monday morning. That same morning, around a quarter of nine, Barbara was waiting as usual at the Jackson Heights subway station for the E train, which is how she traveled to the office. It was a little after the rush hour, so the platform wasn't crowded. Apparently, she was reading the paper. Just as the train was pulling into the station a man, horribly dirty and disheveled—the eyewitnesses agree that he was white, a big, heavy man—yelling or chanting at the top of his voice, ran toward her at full speed, someone said like a football player going for a touchdown, and shoved her onto the tracks just ahead of the train. She was killed instantly.

Good God, I said. Did anyone try to stop him? Was he caught?

No. I guess everybody was stunned, and he ran away just

as quickly—not that anyone was chasing him. Plain disappeared. There is no surveillance camera there, there isn't a better description than the one I just gave you, and there aren't any suspects. According to the papers, the police are doing everything they should be doing, the mayor has offered a fifty-thousand-dollar reward for information leading to an arrest, and so forth.

Was there a service for her? Does she have any family? I'd known her since I was a little boy, but I guess I've never known anything about her personal life. She was just Miss Diamond at first and then Barbara. . . .

There is a younger brother in Florida. Nobody else. He organized a reception at a funeral home in Jackson Heights. I went and so did a lot of other people from the firm. Everybody loved her. She was also cremated.

A grisly coincidence, I said, those deaths. It's as though a single evil force had pursued them.

I didn't want to say so to Kerry, who was already upset enough, but although I had no other explanation I was not ready to accept that the coupling of two such unusual deaths was fortuitous.

After some minutes' silence, during which we ate our sushi and drank the miso soup, I said to Kerry that a thought had been forming in my mind that was rapidly becoming a conviction: the awful story she'd been telling me made no sense. Why would Harry have killed himself? You've told me he was in good health. So it wasn't leukemia or cancer of the pancreas or anything of that sort. You'd talked at various times about pressures he'd been under, and that he'd suddenly retired. That by the way is a real surprise too. But he was a very sane, a very clearheaded, guy. He had plenty of money. It was managed by a very able, very solid investment adviser. I know that, because Harry fixed me up with him. All right, perhaps there were other worries, other forces, that tipped him over into depression. Depression deep enough and painful enough to lead him to hang himself. That is at least conceivable, and perhaps when you tell me about the pressures on him I will see how that could have been. But my mind boggles at the idea that Harry—the gentlest of men—would have killed Plato. Why? Why would he have done a thing like that? He couldn't have been worried about who'd take care of the kitty after he died. Mary would have been delighted to take him. I would have taken him. If he had some crazy idea that there was no one who could be trusted—an absurd idea that wouldn't have occurred to Harry—in that worst case I guess he could have had him put down. But this? Wringing Plato's neck?

She stared at me vacantly. Finally she shook her head and said, I hear what you're saying. I can't understand the part about the cat either. I think I can tell you something about the pressures on Harry, but it's a long story. I don't think I should even try to begin it now. There are some things I must attend to at the office.

I've already heard more than I can absorb, and I too have to go to the office. I have a date with Fred Minot. Let's walk over there together. Are you free this evening? Could we have dinner? I didn't sleep much on the plane, but after Minot I'll catch a nap, and I promise to be fresh as a rose.

I'd rather we went to the office separately. But come to my place at nine. We'll have a simple meal, probably something I'll order in. The introduction to the marvels of my haute cuisine will have to wait.

I'd been cooling my heels in the reception area a good fifteen minutes before Fred Minot's secretary came to lead me to his office and suggested I make myself at home. I sat down on the sofa. It was a large room, though not nearly so large as Harry's corner office, and, unlike Harry's, which, except for his desk, was modern and utilitarian, furnished with too many copies of heavy nineteenth-century furniture. Desk, two worktables, straight-back chairs, and armchairs, in addition to the horsehair sofa. Displayed on the bookshelves and walls were photographs of many blond children swimming, playing football, and skiing, and of a handsome hard-faced blonde woman I took to be Minot's wife. I examined them with interest, my previous encounters with Minot, when I consulted him about my will and when I came in to sign it, having taken place in a conference room. Perhaps another ten minutes passed before he appeared. He was blond as well and large and wore a double-breasted navy-blue pinstripe suit that had surely been made for him by a bespoke English tailor. I remembered the booming voice when he greeted me saying, Sorry to have kept you waiting. I was with Will Hobson, our chairman. He hopes you will be able to stop by to see him after we've finished.

I replied that I would be glad to do so.

Good, said Minot. Apart from the unpleasant circumstances of your uncle's death, the situation is straightforward. Here is a copy of the last will and testament. You will see that, as I told you over the telephone, he has left all his property to you. The bequests that come ahead of you are minor: Harvard College; Harvard Law School; Mrs. Jeanette Truman, the housekeeper at the Fifth Avenue apartment; Mrs. Mary Murphy, the housekeeper in Sag Harbor; the church in Sag Harbor where the memorial service took place; Barbara Diamond, his secretary, but she did not survive him within the meaning of the terms of your uncle's will so that bequest fails; and Mr. José Rodriguez, the handyman in Sag Harbor. In total these amount to two hundred sixty thousand dollars. The assets are your uncle's very substantial investment account managed by Bartleby Associates; his capital account in this firm, between two and a half and three million dollars, which Will Hobson just informed me will be paid out in a lump sum on the first day of next month instead of the usual two annual installments; cash in checking and money market accounts; the Fifth Avenue apartment; the Sag Harbor house; and a very substantial IRA. That's a tax-advantaged savings and investment account. If I understand correctly, your earnings from your books and the film based on your first book have been considerable. With this legacy, it is fair to say you will be very well-off indeed. Of course, even with the current five-million-dollar federal exemption, significant federal and New York State estate taxes will be due, and you may decide to raise cash to pay them by selling the apartment. As you doubtless know, it's very valuable. So is the house in Sag Harbor. You may wish to sell it too. In view of the unpleasant circumstances, your absence, and the need to pay the salaries of your uncle's staff, I secured on an accelerated basis the preliminary appointment as executor under your uncle's will. The salaries have been paid and will continue to be paid until you tell me that Mrs. Truman, Mrs. Murphy, or Mr. Rodriguez should be terminated.

I don't want to terminate anyone, I said. I'd like to leave all the arrangements as they are. Should I now begin to pay the salaries? How does that work?

The estate can continue to pay them, Minot told me. Are there any other questions or requests before you see Will Hobson?

I do have a request, I said. I'd be grateful to you for arranging to have my uncle's personal papers sent to my uncle's apartment. There are also things in his office—photographs, a couple of works of art, and I believe the desk that belonged to my grandfather—that I would ask you to send, also to my uncle's apartment. I'll be glad to pay the movers. And I do have a question. You've said that you have been appointed executor.

Minot interrupted me. No, I've secured a preliminary appointment.

All right, I continued. At some point you might explain to me the difference. But I'm concerned about something else. My uncle told me before I left for South America that you had been named his executor in his will, but he had recently executed a codicil canceling that provision and naming me his executor. Isn't that right? I remember the conversation distinctly.

How extraordinary, Minot said with irritation he didn't try to conceal. I did not see any such codicil in the envelope containing your uncle's will when we removed it from the vault the firm maintains at its bank. We will verify that immediately.

He pressed a button on his telephone. When his secretary appeared, he said, Loretta, please bring the envelope with Mr. Dana's last will and testament.

It was a yellow envelope with Harry's name and what I assumed was a file number written on it. Minot opened it and removed three documents.

There you are, he said. The will, the first codicil adding the bequest to Mr. Rodriguez, and the second codicil that revoked a gift to the Council on Foreign Relations just after your uncle resigned from that organization. There is no codicil substituting you for me as executor.

That's odd, I said. I'm pretty sure I have a copy of the codicil in my files, together with a letter from my uncle informing me that he had signed it and that it was in your possession. Could it have been misfiled? Perhaps you'll be good enough to look into this. At your convenience, of course. What is the next step for the estate?

Apparently unable to form full sentences, Minot answered: Confirm the appointment of the executor. Prepare the estate's tax returns. All in the works.

As we were saying goodbye, I asked whether I could count on him to send the items I had asked for—Harry's personal papers and those few items from his office—to his Fifth Avenue apartment.

I've taken note of what you want from your uncle's office and that should be no problem. Someone will let you know when to expect their arrival. The question of his papers is one you will have to take up with Will Hobson.

Minot's secretary took me back to the reception area. After another ten- or fifteen-minute wait, during which time I supposed Minot conferred with Hobson in person or over the telephone, I saw Hobson emerge from the elevator. He strode toward me, shook my hand, and, calling me Jack, told me he was sorry about my terrible loss. It would be useful to have a talk, he continued. Can you spare the time? Yes? Then let's go up to my office.

We didn't speak in the elevator—I recalled with a pang of grief Harry's chuckling over Mr. Whetstone's rule that conversations in the elevator were to be eschewed because *everybody* eavesdrops—and remained silent until we got to Hobson's office. Once there, he pointed to one of the two chairs facing his desk, closed the door, sat down in the other one, and said: Fred Minot has reported to me on your meeting. The mix-up concerning the codicil to your uncle's will is regrettable. Such things shouldn't happen, but unfortunately they do. However, no harm has been done, and perhaps some good. You've refreshed Fred's memory, and he will take the necessary steps to have you take over as executor. The surrogate's court in New York County is extremely busy, and Fred tells me that process may require as much as three or four weeks to complete. I suggest, if you agree, that Fred should as a matter of convenience continue as the preliminary executor until you qualify. That way the staff's salaries, maintenance charges, utilities, and so forth can be paid from your uncle's checking account, and there is someone in a position to sign such things as social security forms. Do you agree?

I nodded.

Good, Hobson said. I believe that Fred told you that the firm will pay out your uncle's share of its capital in a lump sum. We've decided to waive the usual rules. I trust that's satisfactory.

I nodded again, and thanked him.

Then there is the question of your legal representation, once you qualify as the executor. The normal assumption is that you would ask this firm, and more specifically Fred, as your uncle's longtime counsel who prepared his estate plan, to represent you. But you are free to retain another lawyer to assist you with the administration of the estate. Have you any thoughts about that subject?

Seeing no reason to disguise my feelings, I told him that the chemistry between Mr. Minot and me wasn't good. Probably, I continued, some of it is due to my being upset, but there it is. So I don't think I'd like to have him as my lawyer. Are you proposing that some other lawyer in the firm could take over from him?

That is certainly a possibility, Hobson answered speaking very slowly, and Fred I believe would accept such an arrangement.

Then let me think about it, I said. I'll let you know my decision before the end of the week.

It was Hobson's turn to nod.

There are a couple of other matters, I went on, if you have another moment for me.

Again Hobson nodded.

Are you aware of anything related to the firm or my uncle Harry's work that would have pushed him to take his life or anyway unbalanced him to a very considerable extent? I find his suicide, and the method he chose, and the absence of any letter of explanation absolutely bewildering. He was in excellent physical health, he had no money problems, he had no emotional involvements that had gone wrong, and when I said goodbye to him some three months ago, before setting out for South America, he was in a fine frame of mind. What could have happened?

Hobson recrossed his long legs, seemed lost for a moment in the study of his beautifully polished wingtips, and rubbed his hands as though to warm them.

Jack, he said, it pains me to say so, but Harry had been losing his edge. Nothing one would necessarily remark upon in ordinary life, but the practice of law at the highest level—and that was Harry's practice—makes demands that have no parallel. A man may be the most charming of uncles, dinner companions, and so forth, appear able to hold his own in conversation, and at the same time secretly founder when it comes to finding solutions to complex legal problems or squeezing the meaning out of vast troves of information. Those working with him eventually notice. More painful yet, the poor fellow to whom this is happening comes to be aware of it as well. It's a process that can be slower than the motion of a glacier. But it can also accelerate suddenly, for no ostensible reason. In Harry's case the situation became apparent to his principal client, a client let it be clearly understood of great importance to the firm, none other than Abner Brown himself. To such an extent that some weeks before you left on your well-deserved holiday Abner found it necessary to come to see me and state that he no longer wished your uncle to work on his matters. He cited instances in which Harry's judgment had been seriously clouded and his emotional equilibrium appeared doubtful. As you can imagine this was a shocking revelation and a terrible blow to me on a personal level—Harry and I were taken into the firm the same year—and from the point of the firm. The Brown business accounts for a large percentage of our gross and keeps many partners and associates busy. I was fearful that Abner would announce a withdrawal of all that work from the firm or in any event a substantial part. As it turned out, I was able to avert that disaster. Abner accepted my proposal that I take over Harry's responsibilities. I made the proposal because I thought I must, even though combining Abner's work with my responsibilities as the firm's chairman hasn't been easy and won't get any easier. It was part of that arrangement, I am sorry to say, that I agreed to break the news to Harry and explain to him the reason. Abner didn't have the courage to do it—or perhaps he thought that it would be easier for Harry if I were the messenger. So that's what I did. It was one of the hardest missions I've had to undertake in my life. Harry was devastated. I urged him to seek the help of a first-rate neurologist to deal with the physical aspect, and a psychiatrist to help him on the emotional plane, and I made recommendations as to the doctors, but I don't know whether he followed through. I also pleaded with him—the word is not too strong—not to seek out Abner, not to expose himself to a disappointed client's bitterness. I know for a fact that he disregarded that advice and went out to Houston to see Abner. I have Abner's version of what transpired, which as you will appreciate I'm not at liberty to share with you. I will only add that I told Harry it was necessary for him to retire—at the latest as of the first day of the new year so as to make a clean break. It was in everybody's interest. He had not yet reached the age at which he could do so and receive full pension, but I assured him that the firm would waive the full-vesting rule so that from a financial point of view he would be just fine. To sum up, my dear Jack, I'm afraid that there were circumstances that may explain what Harry did. Especially if he did not consult a psychiatrist, if nothing had been done to lighten his mood, to get him out of the pit of depression.

How horrible! I said. So it looks as though Abner Brown and the firm may have combined to kill Harry.

Hobson turned purple and rose from his chair. I resent that! he shouted. How dare you! Take that back at once and apologize!

I rose as well and said, I do take it back. I should have said that it looks as though your decisions had caused him to kill himself. You've said as much yourself, in somewhat different words.

Hobson sat down, and so did I.

Did Harry continue to come to the office after you had that conversation? I asked, judging that I could take advantage of a temporary cease-fire. Did he accede to your order—or request—that he retire?

Yes to both questions. He did come to the office and

disengaged—quite successfully—from his other client assignments. He did retire as of the first of this year, so that when he killed himself he was a retired partner. The decision to retire made it easier of course to explain to his non-Brown clients why he was reassigning their matters. I should add, Jack, and this is important, that nobody in the firm except my deputy and one partner helping me on the Brown matters knows about Harry's dementia. I thought it was best for him and for the firm to keep that quiet. As you can imagine, there are serious liability issues. Lawyers' mistakes are like time bombs. They explode and come to light unexpectedly. If Harry's condition were known, there could be difficult questions raised as to when the firm's management became aware of it, what kind of supervision we exercised, and on and on. His condition would also weigh heavily on the issue of negligence. Those considerations are naturally in addition to our respect for Harry's privacy and dignity.

And Mr. Minot, I asked, did he know?

Not even he.

I nodded and said, There is an awful lot here for me to think about and grieve for. There is another thing I want to mention. It's Harry's personal papers. I asked Mr. Minot to have them sent to me and he said that was a request I should make to you. I really would like to have them.

My dear Jack, Hobson replied, a form of address that surprised me considering my very recent outburst, we have been through Harry's files. There are no papers in them that are, as you put it, personal. All his papers relate directly or indirectly to his office work and as such are the firm's property.

Most of them are also covered by client privilege that would preclude their release to you even if the firm otherwise wished to hand them over. I must disappoint you.

But that can't be! I exclaimed. For instance my letters to him. My parents' letters to him. His correspondence with friends, with the women who were an important part of his life. I have always understood that they were in the office, in the files maintained by Miss Diamond.

Another tragedy, said Hobson. All I can tell you is that those letters aren't here. He must have removed them, once he understood that he was leaving the firm. Perhaps you had better look for them at his apartment, or in the Sag Harbor house.

He stood up and held out his hand.

I shook it and was almost out the door when he called out: Don't forget to let me know whether you want us to represent you!

V

Jeanette was at my apartment when I got there and began to cry as soon as she saw me.

Welcome home, Captain Jack, she exclaimed between sobs that shook her large and robust frame as I embraced her. I was beginning to think you'd never return. Poor Mr. Harry! Who could have imagined such an end? I've been praying for his soul, but it's no good. He comes to me in my dreams looking just the same as always, only so sad and kind of lost. I've never been so lonely, not since my Walter died.

Walter was her late husband, an army master sergeant, killed in the first year of the Iraq War by an IED that ripped apart him, another NCO, and the driver, as well as the Humvee in which they were riding. I did not think I should remind her that in fact I had written down the date of my return and posted it on the bulletin board in the kitchen.

What's going to become of me after all these years with Mr. Harry? she wailed.

I gave her another hug and said, Shush, I'm awfully sad too, but it's going to be all right for you, you'll see.

The fact was that I had just made an impulsive decision I knew I wouldn't go back on. Fuck Minot and estate taxes. So he thought that my earnings from my books and film had been considerable! The condescending creep didn't begin to know how much money I'd made. I knew I could manage what I was undertaking.

No one will ever replace my uncle, I told her. It can't be. But you and I will soldier on. Uncle has left me the Fifth Avenue apartment. I'm going to move into it just as soon as you and I pack up here, and I hope that you'll stay with me. Same deal as with Uncle Harry. Is that something you want to do? Before you answer, you should know that Uncle left you a nice present under his will. The lawyer at the law firm, Mr. Minot, who prepared the will, told me. So what do you think? Do you want to go on taking care of a rascal like me?

Captain Jack, she replied, you're the best. I'll look after you as long as you want me and my old legs carry me. First thing I'm going to do is make you a nice cup of coffee.

She had already unpacked the duffel bag I'd dropped off on the way from the airport before meeting Kerry, so while she fussed about the coffee I was able to sit down at my desk and look at the accumulated mail. There was a lot of it, almost all consigned by Jeanette to the junk mail category. I rummaged through the stack and agreed with her judgments. Appeals for money from causes I didn't support, offers to buy my apartment, prospectuses for snake oil. In the other tiny stack were also appeals for money from my prep school and Yale, a package sent by Felicity containing a Christmas card and photos she'd taken on her family vacation in Kitzbühel, and routine correspondence from my literary agent. Books one and two were selling briskly. I'd already received bonus payments on account of the film's gross receipts in the U.S. and at this rate it looked as though my tiny percentage of the net would kick in. The interest in book number three was very lively. When would it be finished?

When Jeanette brought in the coffee and slices of pound cake—she told me she'd baked it as soon as Kerry called and said I'd be home the next morning—I asked her to sit down, inquired about her daughters and grandchildren, and moved on to the subject that was gnawing at me. I decided to approach it obliquely and asked first whether Mr. Minot had paid her everything she was owed, including reimbursement for supplies and food.

Oh yes, Mr. Jack, she told me, he came to the apartment several times, asked for the accounts, and paid me right away. He's a nice gentleman.

Her answer gave me the opening I needed.

That's excellent, I said, did he come to get Uncle's mail? Or was there anything else?

Oh yes, she told me, the mail was picked up regularly, by him, his secretary, or a young lawyer, oh yes, once a week. But Mr. Minot didn't bother much with that. He said he needed to go through Mr. Harry's papers for things that had to do with Mr. Harry's property and taxes, and he spent quite a lot of time doing that, looking at Mr. Harry's files in the library and in the desk in the master bedroom. He said he also needed to check Mr. Harry's computer. He took it back to the office with him, and the secretary brought it back a few days later. There was also a problem with the safe. Mr. Minot asked if I knew the combination. I said that I sure didn't, so he came the next day with a technician who worked on it maybe an hour before he got it open. That's when Mr. Minot called me in and asked me to stay in the library so that I would see they only looked for papers and didn't touch any of the jewelry boxes that were there.

I felt both disgust and relief. Those boxes held my grandmother's jewelry, which Harry had told me he was keeping for my wife.

And were there any papers? I asked.

Only Mr. Harry's passport, she told me, and envelopes with cash. Dollars, and some foreign money. Mr. Harry always said he wanted to have cash around in case there was another big power failure or another 9/11 and he couldn't get money out of the ATM. They left everything right there and closed the safe.

I see, I said. And what about the other papers they had looked at. Did they take any of them away?

She shook her head. I'm really sorry, but I can't tell, Captain Jack. I didn't stay with them all the time.

Of course, you didn't, I told her. You've had a terrible time, Jeanette. I now wish with all my heart I had stayed in New York. I wish I hadn't gone on that stupid trip. Perhaps Uncle Harry would still be alive. I try and try, but I just can't get it into my head that he took his own life. Do you think there was something the matter with him, some health problem that had come up? Some other reason? I wish I could understand!

Don't you go and blame yourself, Captain Jack, she answered. It was God's will, not something you could have prevented. Mr. Harry was just fine. He wasn't sick or anything. He told me it made him sad to retire, because he'd miss the firm and the nice young people he worked with, but he'd been thinking and decided that forty-two years on the job was long enough. He had enough money. He wanted to travel. Oh, and God bless him he had another idea: he said he was going to go back to the piano. He hadn't touched that piano in the living room for thirty years, but he was going to take lessons and learn once again to play it good. So he even had it tuned. So like I say, there was no reason for him to do a thing like that. It was God's will.

Or the devil's, I thought.

All right, Jeanette, I said, I guess you're right. I'm dead tired from the plane and from everything I've heard today about Uncle Harry. I'm going to hit the sack for a couple of hours, and then I'm going to have dinner with Kerry Black.

Miss Kerry! Mr. Harry sure loved her! Jeanette interjected. You give her a big hug from me.

That's right, I said, he did, and I will give her the biggest hug I know how. Please keep coming here this week as usual. We'll start packing. I'd like to move to Fifth Avenue next week.

It was almost eight when I woke from a dreamless sleep. I made tea, drank two cups so hot they burned my mouth, and ate another slice of Jeanette's cake. Then I called Scott on his cell phone. Although he was still at the office, he answered right away. I told him briefly what had happened.

You poor bastard, he said. What a mess to come home to! Would you like to take a break and come down to D.C. for the weekend?

I thanked him and said that the mess was one I had to come to grips with, the sooner the better. If I went anywhere it would be to Sag Harbor, as part of dealing with the mess. But I wanted a rain check for D.C.

It's yours, he told me, and it's renewable.

And would you consider coming to the city or possibly Sag Harbor? I may ask you to do that.

The answer was yes, as I had expected.

I took stock. Scott and Kerry, my old prep school and Yalie pal and my uncle's favorite associate and most recently his partner. It might not seem like much, but I thought that the quality of those two made up for the tenuousness of my ties to Kerry—a condition I hoped to remedy soon—and for the narrowness of my circle of friendships. The truth was anyway there was no one else I would want to ask for help, and no one else I wanted to see. In the midst of misfortune, I considered myself lucky.

The Korean on Lexington Avenue between Seventy-Eighth and Seventy-Ninth Streets was open. He sold good flowers. Jeanette got them there for Fifth Avenue unless Harry had ordered an arrangement from his preferred florist, across the avenue from the Korean. I picked up fifteen yellow roses—thus sparing Kerry, I thought, the need to interpret the statement she might have thought I was making if the roses I brought were red—and at five past nine rang her doorbell.

That she too attached importance to my visit became apparent to me as soon as she opened the door and I saw that she had changed into a long sheath of blue-and-green Indian silk and gold lamé ballet slippers. Instead of the habitual chignon, her hair was down, almost to her shoulders. For the first time I noticed that she had big feet—big even for such a tall girl—and unaccountably I found that touching. It was just possible that in this day of outrageous women's shoes, designed to compel attention, they were not her favorite feature. Not to worry: I was willing to adopt them. The impression that she had made an effort was confirmed, and my trepidation grew, when I followed her into the living room. Everywhere, it seemed, on the coffee table, on the table in the dining room area, on the window ledge, stood vases of yellow and pink tulips. She would have gotten them on her way home from the office. Perhaps, if she had picked up groceries, she'd had to make two trips. I didn't think it likely that this overworked Jones & Whetstone junior partner regularly turned her apartment into a lush bower—I didn't recall seeing any flowers at the time of my previous visit—or set her table for dinner with what I recognized was sterling silver and cut-crystal glasses.

This is so beautiful, Kerry, I said, and you are beautiful. Breathtakingly so.

I want to be, she answered smiling. I want you to like me. And I want to give you a drink.

It turned out that we both wanted a vodka. She kept it in the freezer and showed me the bottle. Luksusowa, she said, Polish potato vodka, remarkably good and remarkably inexpensive. A boyfriend I had when I was at the U.S. Attorney's Office put me on to it and even taught me how to pronounce the name. It's the best thing he ever did for me.

The past tense saves the situation, I told her. Have you got a boyfriend now, vodka drinking or other?

She shook her head.

Good, I said, because I want to apply for the position.

The words left my mouth as though they had a will of their own, and I realized that this was not mere banter. Although I hardly knew her, there was something about this girl's nearness—we were sitting on the sofa—that was making my heart pound and filling me with something like joy. A kind of joy that I would not have thought possible with the circumstances of Harry's death as the great subject we would inevitably have to deal with. Except that it was not unlike the joy, triumphant joy, I had felt after the first night during the Phantom Fury in Fallujah, when I realized that no one in my platoon had been hit, or again when the morphine kicked in at Delaram and medics strapped me onto the stretcher for loading on the helicopter, and I realized I was going to live. Where had I been, what had I been thinking of? Why hadn't our few previous contacts been sufficient? Could it be that her being Harry's favorite associate and protégée, perhaps his dream daughter, had prevented me from responding to her as a woman?

As it happens, she told me, the position is open, and a priori you seem qualified. Of course, the matter will have to be investigated.

And there aren't any temps hanging around?

Jesus, she said, you want the terrain all to yourself!

Of course, I said. It's basic infantry tactics: occupy the terrain and secure the perimeter.

You can relax, Captain, she answered, it's a tenure-track position. Applications from temps and adjuncts are discouraged. No, she added seeing me move toward her, don't advance too quickly. Let's drink our vodka and eat the canapés I've prepared. You shouldn't drink vodka without food.

She'd kicked off her slippers and walked to the kitchen barefoot. I took that as an incontrovertible sign of trust. She wasn't going to hide her feet from me. It was a very quick trip. She put on the coffee table a green rectangular dish on which she'd arranged little squares of *pâté de campagne,* each with its own toothpick. They were surrounded by black olives.

For the second time in such a short while I was deeply moved. This was the way my beautiful mother had served hors d'oeuvres, with the same simplicity and care. Why hadn't Harry mentioned her domestic talents? Perhaps he had never had occasion to discover them.

I told her I loved her pâté and olives and managed to restrain myself from saying that I thought I loved her too— or even that I was falling in love.

Good, she said, now we have to talk about Harry. I'm a night person, so if you've gotten some rest before coming over, we aren't pressed for time.

She shifted her position on the sofa and stretched out her legs, so that her naked feet were inches from my left hand.

A knot had formed in my throat, but I nodded and told her, on the whole coherently, the gist of my conversations with Minot, Hobson, and, finally, Jeanette.

She let out a groan. That's just about what I expected. No, it's even more slimy than what I thought those guys were capable of. There was nothing wrong with Harry's mind. I would have been the first to notice. It's a poisonous invention of Hobson's and I don't know who else. He told you they were keeping the dementia a secret. That's the party line and a total fabrication. In fact, they leaked it all over the firm. Not to me, because Hobson knows I'd have laughed in his face or perhaps slugged him, but widely enough for several partners to have come to ask me about it. You know: how bad was it, when did I first notice it, what did I do to make sure that we didn't make mistakes and so on.

And what did you say?

I said that so far as I was concerned there was absolutely nothing wrong with Harry's mind or emotional equilibrium—yes, that was a part of the story, that the clouding of his mind had affected his emotional balance.

And these were all one-on-one conversations? That's all? You didn't speak up? You didn't tell Harry about it? Challenge Hobson? Send around a memo to partners?

I didn't want to embarrass Harry. He was still coming to the office. Practically every day. And then, she suddenly wailed: Jack, there is something you don't know about me that I have to tell you. I was a coward. I hope you will understand the reasons and that they won't make you withdraw your application. It would make me horribly sad if you did.

Nothing you can tell me will have that effect, I said, and,

ready to withdraw at the slightest sign that I had given offense, extended my hand and began caressing those poor shy feet.

The feet were not withdrawn. Instead, they began to rub against my hand in a gesture that made me think of Plato rubbing his back against my leg when he was pleased or wanted to remind me that there was something he'd demanded and I had foolishly forgotten to take care of.

Promise? she asked.

I nodded.

Here is the truth then, she said, the awful disabling truth. Jack, I haven't been able to be brave in Harry's defense, and I can't be very brave now. I have to be extremely careful in my dealings with those pricks because I am so vulnerable. Not even Harry knew about it. But you will. I'm an only child. My parents were in their late thirties when they had me. They were both high school teachers, in Montclair, New Jersey, where we lived. They're both still alive, my mother in a retirement community, my father in a nursing home with a special facility for demented patients. You see, I know about dementia. He has Alzheimer's, has had it for more than ten years. It was slow moving at first. My mother tried to have him at home far longer than was good for her or, indirectly, for me, but about six years ago he got too difficult for her to control, even with the help of a nurse. He made her life hell. So she finally agreed to institutionalize him. The facility is very good and as you would expect very expensive. It's near Montclair. My mother drives there to see him practically every day. That too is hell. Of course the little money they inherited from my paternal grandparents and their savings have been spent. I paid for my mother to get into the retirement community and I give her the extra money she needs for upkeep of the car, clothes, hairdresser, and occasional trips to Princeton or New York that the retirement home organizes. And the presents she likes to give, including presents for me! And I pay for the nursing home. It hasn't been easy, coming on top of what I owed for student loans. By the way, that's why I didn't stay at the U.S. Attorney's Office. I loved the moral clarity of the work I did as a prosecutor— there was never any question about whether I was on the right side when I was putting bad guys behind bars—but I needed the big law-firm salary. And now I can't afford, I can't risk, being pushed out of the firm. It's shameful, but there it is. I can't put my parents in jeopardy so I have to pussyfoot around those guys. I can't be as brave as I'd like. Besides, I like to live nicely. I don't hide it.

She motioned vaguely to show that she meant her apartment. I nodded, and she added quickly, Don't get me wrong, this apartment is anything but expensive. It's rent controlled. You wouldn't believe it, but the building belongs to the Rubinstein brothers. They're a big real estate family in New York, and they've never tried to turn it into condominiums or co-op apartments. Instead they rent to family friends and retainers. I qualified because I roomed with a Rubinstein daughter the whole time we were together at Dartmouth.

Kerry, I said, you're incredibly brave. Telling me took real courage. It's true that we have a lot of disagreeable stuff to talk about, but I am a night person too, so we have lots of time. Do you think you could interview me for my new job before we talk about Harry? Don't keep me on tenterhooks! I need to know I've been hired.

I had not been with a woman, not since the English girl who reminded me of Felicity, and I wanted Kerry desperately. Nonetheless, after I had helped her out of the silk sheath and her modest good-girl panties and bra, and had torn off my own clothes, and we had finally lain down on her surprisingly large bed, I found that instead of needing to take her at once I preferred to touch and explore every square inch and crevice of her muscular and supple body and to breathe in its aroma, a witch's brew of soap, toothpaste, and scents compounded of fresh sweat and intoxicating secretions. She wore no perfume. When, at my urging, she raised her knees, I put my face where I could taste her best. Her moans turned into rhythmic shrieks. Sometime later— but how much later was it?—she pushed me away, and whispered, Jack, don't make me wait any longer, come inside, I want you inside.

I'm unequipped, I too whispered. I hadn't thought . . .

So am I, she whispered back, but it's all right. I've just had my period. Come, my love, come.

She'd actually said it!

We made love twice more and fell into a deep sleep. When I awoke, finding her arm wrapped around my torso, I thought it was morning, but the radio clock told me we hadn't slept more than three-quarters of an hour. We took a shower together. Laughing like a madwoman, Kerry produced from a closet a long yellow peignoir she'd brought home from a Puerto Rican vacation and said she wanted me to wear it to dinner, instead of my clothes, which were so much more difficult to get out of. She'd wear the black one. This was easy, but there was nothing she could ask to which I wouldn't have agreed.

The job is yours, she said, when we sat down to dinner. The requirements are simple: unless I give you the night off, you are required to make me feel just the way you made me feel just now every night of the week. For your information, tomorrow I'm going on the pill, so there'll be no excuses.

The meal consisted of a white gazpacho followed by a shrimp quiche she heated up in the microwave oven and cheese and grapes for dessert. She opened a bottle of Sancerre. We were ravenous, and it wasn't until the cheese and grapes were on the table that I finally brought myself to ask the questions that the "job interview" had put in abeyance. What were the pressures on Harry, I asked, that she had mentioned more than once, and what did she think were the reasons that had led Hobson to force him to retire and invent and spread the lie about his dementia.

There was a long pause.

Look, she said, it all related to Abner Brown and his businesses. Harry had gotten so thoroughly involved in the Brown legal problems, you could say without exaggeration that he alone apart from Abner knew and understood them all, and he'd gotten just as involved with Abner personally. Abner would call him—I don't know—four or five or more times a day. About everything. The troubles with his wife, Linda, the troubles with the constantly changing cast of girlfriends and their demands for money. Money to get them to sleep with him, to get them to go on sleeping with him, to get them to promise not to tell Linda after he'd stopped screwing them. How was he to make these gifts, which ran into many millions a pop, disappear so that Linda wouldn't see them when she signed their joint gift tax return, how to make sure that the bimbo who'd been paid so she wouldn't tell would indeed keep her mouth shut? You know Harry just as well as I, or perhaps better, so I don't need to tell you that this stuff made him sick, but there was no way he could refuse to get involved because it had become a matter of friendship. This is how Abner would put it: You're my best friend, you're my only friend, nobody else can help me out. There were also problems with the boys, the two sons. One of them was caught bugging the headmaster's bedroom at his boarding school. Abner calls Harry: Your grandfather founded that fucking dump! Can you call the fuckhead rector and get him to call off the dogs? You've carte blanche on negotiating the donation. Or, Harry, would you check out triplex X in the new Gehry building, and what do you think of César Pelli's project downtown? There's a penthouse there I might like. Then he'd call in the middle of the night to ask, Have you been to see it yet? Obviously some of it was heady, flattering stuff, and occasionally very interesting. At the same time, Harry observed all the faults, the real baseness and duplicity, of Abner's character and would say to himself, Why did I get sucked into this bog, why didn't I draw the line at representing him and his companies in specific discrete deals? There was no satisfactory answer because the truth was that he did feel flattered and did fall for the lure of the mass of profitable work he'd be bringing to the firm. But then came his increasingly apocalyptic view of the role Abner is playing in the political life of the country through his PACs and his think tanks.

I interrupted saying that I thought he and Abner had agreed right at the outset to keep politics out of their relationship.

He told me the same thing, but that was before Abner burst onto the national scene. At the time, he was only mucking around in Texas and Arizona and spreading his brand of poison through the media. But Harry thought that what he was doing to defeat Obama in the upcoming election was in an altogether-different register. He's subverting the Republic, is what he told me.

Thinking of how the guys in my battalion, officers and NCOs included, had been eating up the shit dished out over the Internet and in talk shows by Abner's Freedom Now Foundation and the talking fuckheads financed by it, I nodded and said, I agree with Harry.

And with me, she replied. Look, Jack, she continued, now we're getting to the pressures that came from Abner's businesses, and here I'm doubly constrained. I've told you, not because I want pity or sympathy, about being vulnerable, which has been for me constraint number one in dealing with what has happened.

Again I interrupted. Kerry, I said, that vulnerability is over. I'll stand with you, at your side, behind you, anywhere you need cover. In practical terms that means that if you need money I'll share my money with you. That's what Harry would have done if you'd only let him, that's what he would have wanted me to do, and that's what I'm determined to do.

She flew to my side of the table, sat down in my lap, and kissed me on my lips. As the kiss deepened I felt an urgent need to get her back on the bed. Talk could wait. My hand under her peignoir, I caressed her breasts until the nipples were hard and she began to grind against me.

Stop, please stop, she said, and moved to the armchair placed catercorner to the sofa. You sit down on the sofa and let me finish what I have to tell you. Before I do, though, I want to thank you. What you've just said is very beautiful and very generous, but I'm a big girl—she giggled—and I have to stand on my own big feet.

The second constraint, she continued, comes from my duties as a lawyer. Canons of professional responsibility. Abner and his businesses were my clients; they are still my clients for those purposes, even though I've been removed from doing any work for them. I can't divulge their secrets, I can't breach their confidences. I've already come pretty close to that when I talked about Abner's personal issues and Harry's involvement in them. This is the constraint that almost drove Harry nuts. So I'm going to talk in generalities. Even that's something I probably have no right to do, but here goes. I believe—but bear in mind that Harry never disclosed to me the facts of his discoveries—that at some point, less than a year ago, when Abner began exploring listing his holding company on the stock exchange, not the very top holding company that owns literally everything in Abner's empire but

the one directly under it that owns the moneymaking businesses, Harry started looking hard at the structure and what
was inside what he called the black box. And I believe that
what he saw curdled his blood. I'm not talking only about
such things as tax evasion, though I'm sure there was plenty
of that, or price-fixing here and there or suppressed or concealed field-test reports indicating that the medical products
sold by some of the Brown companies are dangerous or some
serious pollution and failure to report. No, I believe that he
discovered a pattern of completely pervasive wholesale viola-
tions of law, U.S. law, state law, and laws of the foreign coun-
tries where Brown companies operate. That is what I think
he saw, and the question is what was he going to do about it.
And for God's sake, Jack, remember that he never told me
what he saw or how he got at it. I'm telling you what I believe
happened. He had a problem he couldn't solve.

You know, some obvious solutions occur to me, I answered.
One, he could have gone to the police, the FBI, or whoever
else you go to in such a case. Two, he could have stopped
working for Brown and his companies. And stop dealing with
Abner's personal life! What could have gotten into Harry?

You're right. He could have pulled out. That is the decision
that I think he finally reached, on some such basis as that
Abner and his businesses were engaged in a continuing fraud
and course of criminal conduct, and I think that being a wonderful, hopeless, and lovable stickler for the rules he went to
see Abner in order to "remonstrate" with him. That is what
the ethical canons recommend, if a lawyer intends to quit
working for such a client. Now comes some more guesswork:

once Harry had finished remonstrating, Abner understood that he had grasped the totality of what was going on and was going to withdraw and perhaps also do more. Perhaps he thought Harry had concluded that all the circumstances gave him the right—or even the obligation—to go, for instance, to the FBI. So Abner decided to act preemptively. He hopped on his plane, went to see Hobson, and said, Get Dana off my work. What reasons he gave I cannot tell you because I can't even begin to guess. He's so fucking devious. But I'd bet you what you like that it wasn't a bullshit story like dementia, because Abner knew Harry's mind was fine and that nobody who spent time with Harry would believe that it wasn't!

So you don't think Brown told Hobson that Harry was losing his mind? I asked, beginning to think that I was losing mine. And why would Hobson have come up with it?

Oh Hobson! she said. He didn't want to tell the firm he was kicking Harry out because Brown no longer wanted to work with him, was dissatisfied, or whatever. That would have raised a lot of questions, and if the questions were answered all sorts of stuff Brown didn't like might have come out. So the smear was the solution. Hobson knows the partnership well enough to know that no one would have been comfortable going to Harry to say sorry old friend we're so sad you're out of your fucking mind.

She poured herself some wine.

No, she said, definitely not, Brown didn't come up with that story, although by now he may know about it and may have congratulated Hobson on his brilliant invention. Brown is anything but stupid. Just devious and vicious. I've seen him

a number of times, always with Harry except one time when
I was alone. That exception was a trip I made to Houston
alone in July last year, right after I became a partner. We
met in his office and had a sandwich lunch during which he
talked very broadly, about European history once he found
out that had been my major at Dartmouth and his collection
of Renaissance bronzes, of which he had many on his bookshelves and scattered around on the furniture. We were sitting on a sofa, with the lunch on the coffee table before us.
It'll be a hell of a good lunch, he had told me. He would press
a button, and the waiter would come in and bring dishes and
take away others. He was particularly pleased with his chef's
pecan pie. He kept laughing—an unpleasant sound, let me tell
you—and carried on about how it was forbidden fruit and he
always goes for whatever is forbidden, if I get his meaning. If
it's forbidden, I have to have it. I felt a kind of tension building up, and I was right. As soon as the guy left, having served
the fucking pecan pie and coffee, *wham!* Abner's hand was
on my thigh, making its way up to my crotch. I grabbed it,
and the thought flashed through my mind that I might twist
it and try to break his arm. I'm strong, and physically he's a
wimp, but I chickened out and instead told him, Abner, this
is a really bad idea. I'm your lawyer, remember? He got red in
his face, took his hand away, and said, I can fix that. One telephone call from me will do it. Then he stood up and walked
toward his desk with this huge erection he didn't bother to
hide. Once he'd sat down, he looked at me pityingly and said,
You disappoint me. I thought all Jewesses from New Jersey
like sex. I thought you'd suck my cock! Saying that must have

calmed him, as though he'd shot his wad, because he segued right into our legal business. There was only one interruption. He had his secretary bring a sort of casket and a little gadget he used, after he'd pricked his finger, to test his blood sugar. Then he gave himself an injection. In the tummy. He opened his shirt for that purpose. Then she took the stuff away, including the little swipe he'd used to sterilize the area—he's hairy like an ape—and he said type one diabetes. Pecan pie, my ass! We finished our work exactly on time, he thanked me, and had me driven to the airport!

You've made this up, I told her.

Not in the least. Kerry Black—he figured, because I've got curly black hair and come from Montclair, it's really got to be Kerry Schwartz. The rest is reading *Goodbye, Columbus.* He's got good taste in literature!

I shook my head and probably would have made a speech, but she raised her hand to interrupt me.

Jack, she said, we've gotten sidetracked. I want to explain to you why Harry very likely thought he couldn't go to the police. He would have had to be sure that he met every criterion spelled out in the canons. Believe it or not, that's a tough test to meet, especially for someone like Harry who lived by them.

I do understand that, I told her. Can you tell me how big a role you think the financial considerations played, hanging on to a very big client?

I had a sickening sense that they had been important and wanted desperately to hear Kerry say I was wrong. But she couldn't, not entirely.

I think they played an important role, she answered, but not the way you think. As Harry may have explained to you, we have what's called a lockstep system at the firm. You get paid the same as the other partners of your seniority get paid. It doesn't matter whether you work longer or shorter hours or whether you bring in business, so Harry wouldn't have been focused on the potential impact on his own compensation. But Harry loved the firm. He didn't want to hurt it, or to antagonize his partners by killing the goose that was laying so many golden eggs. And he couldn't tell them all that he knew. That much I'm certain of. Harry made clear to me that his arrangement with Abner was that confidences couldn't be shared with partners or associates except strictly as necessary for completing a particular assignment. And there was one other important factor. Harry was very lonely. Abner kept him busy and amused and made him feel he was a big deal at the firm doing a lot to contribute to its prosperity!

All right, I said, I get it. Or at least I think I get it. Let me try to summarize. You think Harry found evidence of widespread fraud and criminality that pervaded Abner Brown's businesses to the point of being inseparable from them. However, you don't know what that conduct was. Right?

Yes, she nodded.

He decided to withdraw, but first he tried to talk to Abner to get him to reform, come clean, or something like that. There was an implied threat added to it: Otherwise I resign from representing you.

She nodded again.

So Brown decided he'd move first and fire Harry.

I don't know, she said, but that's a good working hypothesis because it makes all of the facts I'm aware of fit together.

All right, let me ask you this: Can you find out for me whether there are indeed no personal papers of Harry's at the firm or, if they do exist, where they are and what has happened to his emails? Does the firm keep copies of its lawyers' emails, and if so would Harry's exist somewhere? I'm focused on this because it seemed so bizarre that Hobson and Minot were eager to get at his papers at the Fifth Avenue apartment and in his safe.

If only Barbara Diamond were alive. Kerry sighed. She would know every detail about Harry's papers and emails.

Well, she isn't, I answered. But you and I are alive, and I have to get to the bottom of what happened. Will you undertake this research for me? I don't want to put you in any jeopardy or make things awkward for you at the firm, but you're the only person I can ask—can you handle it?

Another nod. I'll do my best.

You see, darling, I told her, I'm like a stuck record. I can't bring myself to believe Harry would have killed Plato and hanged himself because he'd lost Abner Brown's business and had been pushed out of the firm. It doesn't add up. Worse—it's utterly inconsistent with everything I know about Harry. There's some other reason, another force at work. I will not rest until I've figured out what that was and what really happened.

VI

raq and Afghanistan had made me a light sleeper. In Iraq, like a lot of my brothers, many nights I was on sleeping pills, counting on the tsunami of adrenaline to flush out all remaining traces of the drug if we came under attack. When I got to Afghanistan, battalion shrinks and medics were handing out antianxiety, antidepression, and antipsychotic mind-fucking medications of every description to troopers like peanuts. I stayed away from them, and, ever since I left the hospital, I've stayed away from painkillers and Ambien and company and have managed to hold insomnia at bay. But luxuriating in Kerry's bed I began to realize that I would need to reach a higher level of mastery over self if I was ever going to get a night's sleep with this big affectionate girl nestling against me when I lay on my side and, when I lay on my back, pinioning my legs under one of hers. As for her, she was out like a light, breathing regularly or snoring or muttering and chuckling to herself. I savored her nearness and my newfound happiness but willy-nilly went over the meetings with Minot and Hobson and what I had learned from Kerry. It became clear to me that the first step in making good on the promise I'd made to her not to rest until I'd figured out what really happened to Harry was to go to Sag Harbor and speak with Harry's housekeeper Mary and his neighbor Sasha. Over breakfast of fresh-squeezed grapefruit juice, soft-boiled eggs, whole wheat toast, and very strong coffee, which Kerry prepared while, at her insistence, I spent an additional twenty minutes in bed, I told her of my plan to go out to Long Island on Saturday morning and asked whether she'd come with me.

I can't, she said, I can't, I'm arguing a motion for summary judgment in federal court on Monday. That means work with the team at the office both Saturday and Sunday. So I'm giving you Saturday night off on condition that you're back in time for a late dinner on Sunday. I'll be bushed and nervous and will need to be pampered!

I called Mary and Sasha as soon as I got back to my apartment. Mary said she could be at the house anytime Saturday morning. I told her that I'd leave the city no later than nine and should be there by eleven-thirty. That was all right with her. When she heard my name, Sasha broke down and cried. She was free on Saturday evening and invited me to dinner at her house. The prospect of speaking with Hobson was repugnant, but it had occurred to me that an official channel of communication with the firm might prove useful. Hobson took my call right away and waited for me to speak. I told him that although I didn't want to have any dealings

with Minot, I hoped the firm would represent me as executor of my uncle's will.

Hobson seemed taken aback. Perhaps he had expected me
to cave and work with Minot after all, but it struck me as
more likely that he had become accustomed to the thought
that I would seek help elsewhere and decided it was good
riddance.

Fred's feelings will be hurt, he said finally, but I suppose
we can't help that. I'm glad you wish to stay with your uncle's
firm. There is a partner I have in mind who'd be a good fit. If
he's available, I'll send you his name and telephone number.

That's good of you, I said. Thinking about what you've told
me about Mr. Brown and my uncle, I've realized that there are
a couple of things that I'm not clear about. Approximately
when was it that Mr. Brown told you he no longer wanted my
uncle to work on his problems, and approximately when did
you tell Harry that he had to retire?

I thought he'd simply hang up. Instead, he said, I've just
looked at my calendar. Abner Brown came to see me on the
fifth of October. He was spending the weekend in the city; I
spoke to Harry the following week. On Tuesday, the ninth, to
be very precise.

The party for my book number two had taken place the
following day, I suddenly realized. So Harry hadn't let on
that he'd just been hit by a truck. And he said nothing during
our dinners in the weeks before I left for Belize. Clearly, he
understood that I wouldn't leave if I knew what was going
on, and he didn't want to spoil a vacation to which he knew I
was looking forward. He was quite a fellow.

I see, I told Hobson, thank you! And if I understand you correctly Harry retired as of the first day of 2012. So from the time you and he spoke until then—or is it until he died—he had the use of his office, Miss Diamond worked for him, and so forth?

That's exactly right, he answered. As I told you, he used that time to disengage from his other client responsibilities and, although I may not have mentioned it, to hand over to me the matters he was working on for Abner Brown. If it hadn't been for the need to do all that, I might have insisted on an earlier retirement date. But you should understand that retired partners, if they wish, may retain an office at the firm—usually a much-smaller office—and the shared services of a secretary who may or may not be their old secretary. We're very civilized, he tittered. Of course, given his worsening condition, physical and psychological, I very much doubt that he would have wished to avail himself of that privilege.

By the time I had hung up with Hobson it was close to eleven. Jeanette had gotten to the apartment before me and was busy packing clothes in preparation for the move to Fifth Avenue. I made sure she had everything she needed for her lunch and mine and set out for a five-mile run in the park. The day had taken shape. After lunch I would work on my book, and at eight I would meet Kerry for dinner at the Italian restaurant to which I had taken Harry on his birthday the day before 9/11. I'd made a Saturday-morning reservation on a Hampton Jitney scheduled to arrive in Sag Harbor at eleven. I could catch it easily if I went to the bus stop straight from Kerry's apartment.

.   .   .

I was so scared, Jack, so scared! Mary said as she embraced me.

I'd been waiting for her in the kitchen of the Sag Harbor house, into which she stormed noisily as soon as she arrived.

You can't imagine what he looked like, hanging there from that rope. He had on one of those flannel shirts he wore around the house, the red one, his old brown corduroy trousers, and socks. I looked for his shoes later, and I found his slippers—you know, those L.L. Bean slippers he wore around the house—put away neatly under the sofa. As though he'd put them there before lying down and then decided to get the ladder and the rope. And his face! Blue-green, with little specks of red, eyes bulging. The smell was something terrible. He'd shat and pissed in his pants. And Plato on the floor a little ways off, his head twisted, like a rag doll's. At first I couldn't believe it. But it was worse than that. When I picked up the poor little thing I saw that his whiskers had been cut off! Can you imagine such a thing? The shears—I guess he did it with the poultry shears—were lying right there on the worktable.

Mary, I said, are you sure? I hadn't heard that before. It's impossible. Harry would never have done such a thing.

I didn't tell Kerry about it because she was already so sick over what happened. I didn't want to make it worse. What can I say? Here, see for yourself. I took pictures.

She took out her cell phone, brought up the picture gallery, and showed me two photos of Plato lying on a towel, his head twisted and, without the slightest doubt, the whiskers shorn off.

Let's sit down, I said, and have a drink. I need one.

She said she could use one too, a gin and tonic. I prepared one for her and poured a triple shot of bourbon over ice for myself.

What did you do with Plato's body? I asked.

I took it to the vet we use and had him cremated. The ashes are waiting for you. I thought you might want to bury them in the flower bed, where he used to lie in ambush waiting for chipmunks. That's if you're keeping the house. If you aren't, Brian and I will bury him in our backyard.

I told her that I planned to keep the house and hoped she'd work for me just as she had for Harry.

You bet I will, she answered.

Good, I said. If you have time we'll have lunch together, but first let's go over everything, I mean everything you saw and did that day when you found the body.

The story she told me was almost word for word what Kerry had said. Then, when we walked through the house—because I wanted to retrace her steps—she added some information that was new. The house when she arrived that Monday morning was neat as a pin. Harry's bed made, the bathroom as though he hadn't used it, the kitchen the same, he'd either had lunch out and hadn't bothered making tea in the afternoon or he'd thrown out the garbage before killing himself—here she choked on tears—because the kitchen pail was empty, and he'd put in a fresh liner. Harry always kept everything in order, but this absence of any sign of his presence although he'd been there since Friday morning was eerie. Of course, she'd been there on Friday and cleaned, but still she'd never seen the house so dead. The ladder he'd used was kept in the garage, so he'd have carried it to the studio.

We went together through the kitchen into the garage to take a look at the ladder. Just as I remembered, it was an eight-foot fiberglass stepladder that Harry had bought at the hardware store on Main Street and was proud of, although he complained about it being just a bit too heavy. Beside it was the six-foot aluminum ladder he used for most purposes. Harry's Audi was in the garage as well, clean but dusty, I noticed.

Which ladder did he use, I asked, although I thought I knew the answer. The big one so he could reach the beam and tie the rope?

No, he didn't, she answered, he used the little guy. He must have stood on top of it. I guess he didn't want to open the garage door and carry the big ladder through the front door into the garden and the studio. He would have never gotten it through the kitchen.

I guess that's right, I said. Do you mind if I take the six-footer to the studio? I just wonder whether I could have tied the rope around the beam standing on it.

She seemed surprised but didn't object.

It made me sick to do it, but I opened the ladder and stood it up in what I supposed was the position Harry had chosen—Mary had pointed to the spot almost precisely in the middle of the room—and climbed up to the top, where the warning labels tell you that you're not supposed to stand.

Harry was almost exactly my height. Perhaps half an inch taller. I lifted my arms.

What kind of rope was it? I asked Mary. Nylon?

No, she said, some kind of hemp.

Thick?

I wouldn't say so, less than an inch.

So it wouldn't be especially heavy.

Harry used to keep his boat at the Three Mile Harbor marina, the Sag Harbor marina not being to his taste, and only gave it up when the traffic on Route 114 between Sag Harbor and East Hampton and then through East Hampton to the boat got bad, and the time it took to go to Three Mile Harbor and back home could no longer be justified. He had been a good sailor when I last had an opportunity to observe him and had a first-rate sense of balance. He should have had no trouble laying the rope over the beam and tying a square knot. Prior to that, he would have tied a hangman's knot at the other end, something every sailor and fisherman knows how to do, and slipped the end he was going to attach to the beam through the loop he'd made. Then he would have gone down a couple of rungs to put the noose around his neck, and at some point—how much time would he take?—kick the ladder away. . . . It occurred to me that it must have been a short rope, or that anyway he'd tied it so there wasn't a big distance between the beam and the noose.

By the way, I asked, where is the rope?

The police took it, she told me. I don't know where they keep evidence, I guess it's evidence, but if you like I can ask my girlfriend to find out. She works at the Southampton station as a dispatcher.

Have you ever seen a length of rope like that in the house? I asked.

She hadn't, she told me, and agreed that it was hard to think of where Harry would have put it away so that she wouldn't find it. Was it possible that he'd bought it at the hardware store on Saturday, the day before? He was well known there. We agreed that we'd stop by after lunch and inquire. Was there another place he might have gone? The answer was obviously yes: the hardware store in East Hampton, another one in Bridgehampton, and the Kmart at the Bridgehampton mall, and perhaps there were ship-supply stores in East Hampton we didn't know about. But why would Harry have avoided the store on Main Street, where he'd been going for more than forty years?

Let's go to lunch, I said. American Hotel? That's surely what Harry would have advised.

The maître d'hôtel had known Harry very well and may have remembered my face from the times I'd come to his establishment with my uncle. I was grateful to him for the silent embrace and the expression of sorrow on his face, which I thought was genuine. I introduced Mary as Harry's dear friend.

I hope we'll go on seeing you often, he answered, leading us to a corner table in the farthest room in back of the bar. This is our quietest table. It's good if you don't want to be disturbed while you talk.

Did the police do any sort of check to see whether there'd been a break-in? I asked Mary after I had thanked him and we had ordered.

Not really, she said. There wasn't any sign of one. The

windows were all closed and latched, as usual in January. No door had been forced. There wouldn't have been any need to. Harry didn't lock the front door while he was in Sag Harbor. He'd lock it before leaving for the city. Or the studio door. In his opinion there was nothing in the house worth the trouble of stealing, not when he was around.

We fell silent, eating the lobster bisque, which had been Harry's winter favorite.

Very strange, I said when I saw that she had finished. Add to that what happened to Plato. Are we supposed to think that Harry, having neatened his bedroom and the kitchen—even though he was going to hang himself—locked the front door, but incompletely? Usually, people want to be found once they're dead, and they lock the door only if they need time to die, for instance if they've taken sleeping pills or cut their wrists. He didn't have that worry, because if you hang yourself you die.

God, Jack! she exclaimed, please stop.

Let me just carry out my thought. Believe me, I'm not some sort of expert on suicides. All right, he knew he'd be found because you were coming in the morning, so he didn't have to leave the front door open. But if he was going to lock the door as though he was going away, why not do it in the usual way? Both locks. And then something else that has been bothering me since I spoke to Kerry on my way back from Brazil: no letter for me! no letter for you! or for Kerry or his friend Sasha, or for Jeanette who'd been with him almost forty years. Nothing! He was probably good and mad at the law firm. . . .

She nodded, and said, Yeah, retiring from the law firm and all that.

But he had no reason to be mad at any of us. So what went through his head?

Stop, Mary said. There is something you don't know, that I didn't tell to that man from Harry's office or to Kerry, and haven't told you until now. There is a letter for you. I didn't want to give it to them or to the police. I wanted to keep it to give it to you when I saw you.

Her backpack was next to her chair. She rummaged in it and extracted with two fingers a Ziploc bag. Inside was a sealed blue envelope I recognized as part of the stationery Harry had used in Sag Harbor. She reached into the back-pack again, got a Kleenex, unzipped the lock, and using the tissue removed the envelope and handed it to me.

I've been careful with it, she said.

Following her example, I slit Harry's envelope open and took out the folded sheet. The envelope was addressed to "My beloved nephew Jack." Both the address and the letter had been written in blue ink, with a ballpoint pen. I had never seen anything, not even a shopping list, written by Harry in blue ink, and he hardly ever used ballpoint pens. Yes, perhaps if he needed to press hard as when he filled out a FedEx shipping label—a rare occurrence, since nor-mally that task was relegated to poor Barbara Diamond—and wanted to make sure that his writing came through on the three or however many carbon copies. For everything else, he used a Waterman fountain pen, so inseparable from him as to seem a part of his anatomy, and the pen was filled with black ink. And to use a blue ballpoint pen to write this letter!

Mary, I asked, I didn't see Harry's fountain pen on the desk in the studio. Have you seen it?

Yes, she said, it was on the desk, and I've put it in the desk drawer.

I see, I answered, and read the letter aloud.

> *Sag Harbor, Sunday, January 8, seven p.m.*
>
> *My Beloved Nephew Jack,*
>
> *As you know, life has weighed heavily on my shoulders for a long time now. The reasons are many, most of them known to you. I have decided that this is the time to act. Guns are messy, and besides, as you know, I don't own one. I have thought of opening my veins, but that's messy too. So this exit seems perfect. For, in the words of Mark Twain—if the desire to kill and the opportunity to kill came always together, who would escape hanging? He! He! He!*
>
> *So goodbye old chap! I wanted to get this done before you returned from Chile. No use in getting you involved in the nitty-gritty of my death.*
>
> *I am leaving to you our family Bible. Treat it with reverence, and do not fail to search it for guidance in your perplexity and anguish.*
>
> *Your devoted uncle,*
>
> *Harry C. Dana*

Jesus! said Mary. That's one weird letter.

Our waiter was hovering at the other end of the room. I called him over, told Mary that I wanted a stiff single-malt scotch and asked what she'd like. It turned out to be an Irish whiskey.

I still have the old country in my bones, she said.

The letter is a joke full of meaning, I told her, a very clever, a diabolically clever, joke. We'll have to puzzle it out.

And then I asked her rapid-fire, because the ideas came crowding at me, what if anything had happened to Harry's papers, if he had any in the house, and to his computer and cell phone.

There was that awful lawyer from Harry's law firm, Piggott or something like that—Minot, I corrected, and she nodded—who came either just before the day of the service or the day after, I can't remember which, said he was the executor, and went through the house looking for correspondence and stuff like that, he told me. I think he said he found what he wanted. You know, Jack, I wasn't in good shape. He also took Harry's BlackBerry, saying it was office property, and Harry's laptop. I told him the laptop was Harry's property, and he said that was right, but he had to see whether there were any client materials on it. He turned it on and tried to look for himself, but he didn't have the password, so he said he was taking it to the technicians at the office who'd figure it out. I told him I wanted the laptop back here as soon as they'd finished. He said he'd FedEx it to my personal address, and that's what he did. A few days later. I've put it back in Harry's bedroom.

But didn't he have an iPhone as well? I asked. He played with it all the time.

That's right, she said. I haven't seen it anywhere. Maybe he left it in the city.

We had another round with our coffee. Neither of us wanted dessert. I told Mary that I'd be back, either the following weekend or the weekend after, and that I hoped to bring Kerry and perhaps a friend from D.C. with whom I'd been at school and at college and that I saw no reason why I shouldn't take Harry's Audi. It would make going back and forth a lot easier, and since we were paying for the garage in the city we might as well use it. As an afterthought I added that I would just as soon she didn't do anything about getting the rope back from the Southampton police or even talk to her girlfriend the dispatcher about it. Let's wait just a bit, I said. There may be other things we'd need her help with. In reality, it had occurred to me that probably the rope was in a plastic bag lying undisturbed in some storage room at the Southampton station and I would rather leave it undisturbed. On our way back to Harry's house, where she'd left her truck, we stopped at the hardware store. The salesman who more or less ran it greeted Mary exuberantly and offered me condolences after she'd introduced me as Harry's nephew and now the owner of the house. After he'd told me how much he looked forward to seeing me as a regular customer in the store, I asked whether he sold hemp rope about one inch in diameter. My request presented no problem for the Main Street hardware store. Several brands were available.

After looking them over, I told the salesman that it had been my impression that my uncle had said he was going to buy several lengths of such a rope, and Mary and I had looked for them in the garage and in the cellar but didn't find them. Did he remember Harry coming in to make such a purchase?

The guy looked at me queerly. I guess I wasn't fooling him

about the reason for my questions, but he wasn't going to wade into such a sensitive subject and put his foot in it.

No, he said, I have no such recollection. Mr. Dana came in several times in December, and I had the pleasure of serving him, but he never made such a purchase. Anyway, I can check.

He went over to the computer on the counter, went through various maneuvers, and came back shaking his head. Nothing like that in the last twelve months.

Perhaps I'll see you next weekend, I told Mary, once we were out in the street. Probably I'll come out on Friday evening, but I'm not sure. I'll give you a call. Let's say goodbye here. I'm not going to walk back to the house with you. I need a breath of fresh air. I think I'll head toward the harbor.

Sure, you'll see me, she answered. I'll be there on Saturday, around ten, to let you sleep in, just like when Harry was alive and only came out on weekends.

Then I called out to her, Mary, did Harry have any enemies around here—you know, people who might turn violent?

She thought for a moment and said no, and then thought some more and said there'd been the Polish carpenter from Springs who'd come last summer and really fucked up the screen doors he was supposed to repair, and Harry had been pretty sarcastic about it. But Harry paid him exactly what the guy wanted and just told him never to show his face around the house again. And an irrigation guy from Hampton Bays. But that was a couple of years ago, and there too Harry paid him. Jack, Harry was a real gent. He paid people on time, and exactly what he'd agreed to pay.

.   .   .

The cloud cover was heavy. Standing at the edge of the Long Wharf, I looked across the empty gray stretch of Peconic Bay toward Shelter Island and resolved to take Kerry there in the spring for a hike through the Mashomack Preserve. That was something I had done every summer as a boy, with Harry or my mother, graduating from the shortest trail of less than a mile when I was six or seven to the grown-up five-mile stretch by the time I was ten. Harry would bring binoculars, brandy in a hip flask, and dark chocolate for me; my mother contented herself with milk chocolate. I hadn't been back since. The marina was desolate too. The smaller boats had all migrated or had been pulled out of the water for the winter. Only big tubs registered in Caribbean tax havens, ugly, dirty, and neglected, were left, moored on the east side of the pier, the crews nowhere in sight. What were they? Excursion boats hired for gambling and sex parties or church-sponsored bingo and canasta? I turned around and walked toward the village and had almost reached the traffic circle, where Main Street meets Route 114, when the smell of fried oysters assailed me. I bought a serving at the window counter, which was dished out on one of those ubiquitous cardboard punts on which everything now seems to be served, and ate the greasy stuff on my way home.

I'd forgotten my cell phone on the table under the mirror in the front hall. There were no messages on it, and there weren't any on the landline answering machine. Kerry must be working hard. I urinated, washed my hands and face, brushed my teeth, and poured myself a glass of Harry's

Macallan whiskey. A tremendous wave of fatigue and disgust was sweeping over me. I carried my drink to the studio, took my socks off, made a pillow out of the silk-and-velvet cushion on the sofa the way I had so often watched Harry do it, and stretched out under the alpaca throw. I didn't bother with an alarm clock. Dinner with Sasha wasn't until eight—Harry's standard hour in the country, she'd said—and I was sure I'd be awake in plenty of time. In fact, I was up in a couple of hours, needing again to pee. What with the wine, coffee, and whiskeys, I'd taken on too much liquid. Sleep eluded me when I lay down again. Tossing and turning, I ran my hand along the ridge between the sofa's middle cushion and its back and felt a rectangular metal object. I fished it out and saw that I was holding in my hand Harry's iPhone. Holy God, I said. And then immediately added, Young Mary doesn't clean as well as she'd like me to think.

I got up, called Mary, got her at the pet shop, told her what I'd found, confessed to the shameful truth that I didn't own an iPhone, and said that the fucking thing wouldn't turn on.

The battery's dead, she pronounced, it figures after all these weeks, and went on to tell me that the power pack for Harry's MacBook wouldn't help, since for some reason it wasn't compatible with the phone. She remembered though that Harry often charged his cell phones in the Audi. The power packs for the BlackBerry and the iPhone might just be there. She was right. The charger was right there, plugged into the cigarette lighter, complete with the USB cable hanging from it. I stuck it into the iPhone and hoped it had started charging. I didn't think it was at one hundred percent by the time I'd taken my bath and put on clean clothes for dinner with Sasha. Anyway, I realized that I had better restrain my impatience to plumb its secrets. If I started messing with it, I'd keep Sasha waiting, which was something I didn't want to do. There were two other problems. I needed a password and had to face the fact that even if somehow I succeeded in opening the iPhone I hadn't the remotest idea about how to get at anything in its bowels that would be of interest. Something told me that I would eventually figure it out, being an inveterate fiddler who habitually puts aside owner's manuals in favor of feeling his way around a machine. I decided I'd begin by calling Kerry. She was in a conference room, rehearsing the argument she'd be making on Monday. We had to be brief. I told her I had one question: Was there a set number of letters or figures one had to use to unlock an iPhone? It depends, she said. For instance, six if it has access to Jones & Whetstone email. Why?

I've found Harry's phone, I told her. We'll talk later. I love you a whole lot.

Just as I was walking out the door, it came to me what the password would be. "Inca." No, six letters, therefore, "myinca." The name of Harry's adored Olga—or Inca—was part of every password on the list Harry had given me when I came to live with him after Walter Reed. He didn't have an iPhone at the time, but I didn't see why this password would be different.

VII

I s it possible to rush through a dinner with a beautiful, gifted, and grief-stricken old lady without giving offense? And to keep up a stream of conversation she clearly likes while concentrating on something else? I think I managed that feat with Sasha, although I must confess that to say I rushed through dinner may be somewhat misleading. I'm naturally a fast eater, and once we were at table I made no effort to slow down. Unable to keep my thoughts away from the cold black rectangular gadget that by now must be fully charged, I poured champagne for her, mixed a martini for myself—So like Harry, she told me, it could be he standing there in your place—and drink in hand followed her into her studio and expressed genuine admiration for her precise, meticulously observed paintings of the fast-disappearing Long Island potato fields and farmhouses, and did justice, both by the speed with which I devoured them and by appreciative comments, to her chicken pot pie and key lime pie, both of which she confessed came from a caterer, and the

Bordeaux, which with tears in her eyes she told me was part of a case Harry had given her for Christmas. But long before we got to dessert, she put to me questions that, judging by her diffidence, had been preying on her mind. Was I going to keep the house and Harry's apartment? I assured her I was. Because, she said, there were so many of her works in both places. Harry had been a generous supporter, such a steady friend, that he probably bought more of them than he really wanted or needed to put on his walls, just to keep her spirits up during a period when painters like her didn't have an easy time selling. Anyway, she would be happy to buy back from me any paintings I thought I didn't want. The essential thing from her point of view was to make sure they had a happy home and avoid their being sold at auction. Sometimes the prices are much too low and other collectors are disappointed and offended!

I assured her that until I went broke I would live in both places, on Fifth Avenue and in Sag Harbor, and that if anything she should think of me as a collector eager to own more of her work. As a matter of fact, I was taking the painting of Harry's house that's now in the dining room to New York, in order to hang it in my study, and would need a new landscape to replace it. And I had questions of my own, about Harry. Was she up to talking about him and what happened?

She nodded and said, We must. Can't be cowards about it.

She had a well-organized mind and excellent memory. There was no doubt in her mind that Harry had been in good health and gave no sign of depression—only cold rage, she said, at being pushed out of the firm before normal retirement by that awful man Hobson.

I happen to know him and that wife of his, who's a bitch, she said. My late husband and he used to play golf in the same foursome in Boca Raton. Tom couldn't stand him either. But Harry was getting over being angry, and he really looked forward to your return. He had some idea that if you made good progress on your book, you and he might go to London together in May and see some plays. Plato would stay with me—he didn't like the idea of his staying at Mary's because of all the other animals.

As for what happened on that Sunday in January, among all the odd, incomprehensible aspects there was this: Harry had actually asked her to go out to dinner with him, and she told him she couldn't because it was the evening that her book club met. So if it's true that he died around seven, that was just when she and her group were discussing *David Copperfield*!

I know it's a stupid thing to think and to say, she continued, but I can't help myself. If only I hadn't had my book club, if I'd gone over to have a drink with him, if we'd gone out to dinner afterward—I think he had in mind the Greek restaurant in Water Mill—he might well be still alive!

I comforted her as best I could and asked if she had observed anything unusual or peculiar before she went out or as she was going out.

Nothing, she answered, really nothing.

Then she shook her head and added: There was this. I came back early. It must have been a little after eight. The house was dark, which probably meant either that Harry was in the studio or that he had gone out and hadn't left the porch light on. Then, as I was getting undressed, I saw lights go on through the house sort of systematically. Beginning in the entry, then the dining room, the kitchen, then the living room, then one after another the upstairs bedrooms. As though Harry had been going through the house looking for something. I might have called him to ask whether he was playing hide-and-seek or something dumb like that—we'd have these silly telephone conversations once in a while— but I was tired and didn't want to bother him. Here, come to the window and look at your house. Now you see that I could observe all this because of the way the houses are angled. God, I wish I had called. For one reason or another he must have been in such despair!

Awful, I said, awful. May I ask one more question? Can you think of anyone who had a real grudge against Harry, who would have wanted to do him harm?

You mean stage a murder as a suicide?

I nodded.

She thought for a while, shook her head as though to clear it, and answered, Really nobody. Nobody. It's the sort of thing that would have had to be done by a local. Is that what you think? None of our friends would seem rough or strong enough to pull that off.

I agreed we could safely exclude Harry's Sag Harbor friends—anyway the ones I had come across.

That does leave the locals, she continued, and really there isn't anyone. You know Harry could be sarcastic, and he certainly could let it be understood when he wasn't pleased with the way things were done. By the way, that wonderful Kerry has told me that was also the way he was at the office. But he never left bills unpaid, he didn't bad-mouth tradesmen, he was superloyal. If he liked a vegetable stand, wild horses couldn't drag him to another. Oh Jack, it's so sad, such a pity.

Superloyal Harry . . . "myinca" worked on the first try. The phone opened, and I immediately realized I had no clear idea of what I was looking for or how to look inside that phone. His address book, in the hope of finding a contact Kerry or I could identify as suspicious? Certainly his calendar. I wanted to verify Hobson's account of when their conversations had taken place, as well as the trip to Houston. I'd no doubt that the calendar was meticulously kept and updated and would contain that information, but I didn't want to risk messing it up. I'd have to learn about this gadget first. Tapping idly on icons that for other reasons aroused my curiosity I opened one called Utilities. Hidden behind it, I finally saw Contacts, which opened to reveal a list so vast and full of names of persons who were almost surely professional connections that I decided I would have to study it with Kerry's help; a calculator, of all things; a compass; and voice memos. I tapped on that icon and brought up the image of what looked to me like an old-fashioned recording-studio microphone. A series of maneuvers, mostly tapping on it, produced nothing, and I began to worry about accidental deletions. Hadn't I better leave the phone to Kerry, who had one and would know how to unlock its secrets? I was seeing her the next evening. Hadn't I done enough and seen enough for one day? Because I couldn't bear to be separated from it, I took the phone with me downstairs to the pantry, poured a whiskey nightcap that was way too big, and carrying it and the phone went to my bedroom—still the guest room across from Harry's—lay down on the bed, and, unable to resist the lure of the mysterious gadget any more than I could keep my fingers out of a bowl of salted cashews, poked at it some more. Suddenly the phone came alive. It began to speak with Harry's voice. I sprang up from the bed only to collapse in the wing chair. With growing horror, which the whiskey could do nothing to still, I listened to my uncle. The sound was very low, but if I strained I could make out every word—or so it seemed to me.

To do tomorrow, he was saying, first, call Edgar and have him check the furnace, I think it's knocking; second, make a lunch date with Jason; third, get tickets for *Rigoletto* and invite . . .

There was a pause of less than a minute, and he was heard again; now his voice was shrill, unnatural.

What is this, who is it? he was crying out.

What is this, who is it? mocked another voice, that of a foreigner who expressed himself in English marked by persistent faults of grammar such as mishandling tenses and dropping the definite and indefinite articles. But the accent didn't make him difficult to understand. As I listened, I realized that I was familiar with patterns of speech that were not dissimilar: those of a doorman, an elevator man, and a porter at Harry's New York building, each one of them from some part of what had once been Yugoslavia, a Kosovar, a Montenegrin, a Bosniak . . . Or was this accent more like that of the Syrian cleaner on Lexington Avenue, who regularly broke the buttons of my suits? Meanwhile the Voice continued inexorably.

Nice place, old man, too bad you got to lose. Let's go, on feet.

The Voice went from mocking to brutal.

Please say who you are and what you want, replied Harry. By the way, you can put that knife away. I'm not going to jump you.

I need knife, said the Voice. I'm butcher.

Please answer my question, Harry persisted. What is it you want?

Nothing. Everything. I don't rob. I kill. I kill you.

I had to admire Harry. Perfectly steady, he replied, Why kill me? If you want money, let's talk about it. Who sent you? If someone's paying you to attack me, I can probably pay more if you leave in peace. Come on, let's talk like grown-up sensible men.

You're piece of dead meat, replied the Voice. Stop bullshit. I don't kill you, my boss kill me. On feet! I need ladder.

There was a short silence and Harry screamed. A sharp, hideous scream of the sort I'd heard in Iraq when some CIA goons were interrogating a Sunni bastard the Iraqi police had turned over.

You like? the voice continued. Want more?

There was another scream, and then a muffled reply. All right, said Harry, the ladders are in the garage.

We go, dead meat!

I wondered suddenly why the autopsy report—at least according to Kerry—had not mentioned signs of violence or a struggle. The guy had clearly hurt Harry badly. Then I remembered that there were skills. Technique. Skills that let you inflict unbearable pain by hitting just so, in just the right place, without breaking anything, organs, bone, or skin.

Sound of steps, the door opening, Harry saying, Now, now, Plato, you're a good kitty, you can go out and play.

But the Voice resumed: Cat stay.

For God's sake, let the cat go out in the yard.

You stupid, dead meat?

Harry screamed again, an even-shriller scream.

Cat stays.

The door slammed. There followed a silence I timed: eleven minutes. Suddenly, I understood. For some reason, most probably by accident, the recording function of the phone had been turned on before the device slipped into the space between the cushions and the back of the sofa. Harry didn't have it with him while he and the Voice went to the garage to get the ladder. Perhaps he'd forgotten it was turned on. Perhaps he didn't know.

The door opened and slammed shut again, the Voice menaced, Cat stays, and I heard a noise I decided was the ladder being dragged along the floor.

Set up here, commanded the voice. See rope? Maybe I don't butcher. Maybe you hang. Climb ladder, dead meat, and tie end on beam. Good knot so you not fall.

Fuck you, Harry answered, you scumbag. Who's your boss? If you're going to kill me I deserve to know.

A scream followed.

You want know name of boss, dead meat? Try to think! Who'd want you dead? Think hard!

There's no one.

No one? You sure? You think hard? Up the ladder, dead meat!

Fuck you, you son of a bitch! You hang yourself! I'm not going up that ladder. Come at me with your fucking knife, come on and try me.

There was no scream that followed. Just steps and Plato's muffled screech. He was a silent cat, never meowing to get your attention. A screech if you wanted to brush him at a time he judged inappropriate or a real howl if you stepped on him or once or twice in my experience when he was sick with an infection and vomited violently. In a moment, I knew the reason: the Voice had picked up Plato, and Plato was protesting.

You like cat? the Voice inquired. Nice cat, huh? You fuck cat, you pervert? You want to see what I do to him if you not behave? You want me show on cat what I can do with you later?

Leave the cat alone, leave the cat alone!

Harry was shouting but also pleading.

Silence. Some sort of shuffling, and Plato's screech the like of which I'd never heard. And over it Harry yelling, Stop, stop, oh my God you've cut his whiskers, I hope you rot in hell.

The Voice, implacable: Dead meat, you want a cat's paw? I cut it for you.

Then Harry: For Christ's sake, stop and let go of my cat. I'm going up your goddamn ladder.

Not so quick, dead meat. Sit. At desk. Take paper, envelope, and write. You write to your nephew, the big-shot marine. You tell him it's time to go.

Plato screamed desperately.

The Voice: You write, dead meat, or I cut cat's tail off.

The Voice again: That's better.

After a silence, the Voice said, Read letter.

I thought I was beyond horror or shame, but suddenly I heard Harry reading aloud haltingly, brokenly, the text of the letter Mary had given me at the American Hotel.

All right, dead meat. Put letter in envelope and start climbing.

I heard what I guessed was Harry's heavy breathing mixed with sobs.

The Voice said: You still fucking around. Put noose on.

There was silence, then Harry screaming, You're killing the cat, over a horrible scream from Plato, and then the sound of what must have been the ladder falling to the ground followed by a thud. That was surely Harry's fall, checked by the rope.

After that nothing except the Voice muttering words I couldn't understand, interspersed with "shit" and "cunt," and the slamming of the door. That meant, I surmised, that the Voice had left the studio and began the peregrination through the house that Sasha had observed.

It wasn't yet eleven. Unless I called Kerry at home right away she might start worrying. About what, I couldn't tell, nor could I be sure that she would in fact worry. Perhaps, like me, she wasn't the anxious type. In any case, if I waited much longer it would be too late to call. I took the phone and the glass with me, returned to the pantry, and poured myself another drink. What could or should I tell her? As she'd said, she was vulnerable, and that was the reality no matter how many one-hundred-percent-sincere speeches I made about being at her side and so forth. Of course, I could leave her money in case something happened to me, and of course I could tide her and her parents over if, like Harry, she was pushed out of the firm. But I didn't think that was all she worried about. The firm was also a big part of her identity, her raison d'être. She'd been made a partner such a short time ago! Was that to be put at risk? Then there was the question of her safety. Was it far-fetched to think that the psychopaths responsible for killing Harry might go after his closest collaborator? I didn't think so, and, in that case, wasn't it necessary to make Kerry aware of what was going on? Get her to take precautions, whatever they might be? Besides, I badly needed her legal advice. To what use could the recording on Harry's phone be put? What should be the next step? The Suffolk County police seemed to be blundering fools. Could we go to the FBI?

I dialed Kerry's home number. She picked up at once, and although her voice was light and happy I thought I could tell she'd been waiting for the telephone to ring. There's an awful lot to tell you about, I said after we'd told each other how much we needed to be together. Wait till tomorrow. Shall I come to get you at eight?

Come at seven, if you can, she answered. We've made great progress at the office. I'll be ready, ready to listen and for you know what.

The other person whose advice, and perhaps help, I needed was Scott Prentice. The SOP was to call his cell-phone number. There was no need to worry about the lateness of the hour, even considering how early people go to bed in D.C. When he didn't want to be disturbed, he turned his phone off. I suspected that there was another phone with another number that was never turned off, the phone on which his colleagues and superiors could reach him at any moment.

He too answered at once.

I've been in Sag Harbor all day, I said, and I'm knee-deep in shit. It's hard to give you an account over the phone, and for one important part we really need to be in the same place. How does next weekend look for a visit to Sag?

Subject to some Pakis I'm interested in, it's good. If the shit is deep though, do you want to wait until then? I'll come for the weekend, but why don't you hop on the shuttle on Monday or Tuesday afternoon? We'll have dinner and talk.

Tuesday, I said. And the weekend too. It's a deal.

After I hung up, I found myself analyzing my feelings. I didn't think I was afraid of the Voice, and had someone asked me I would have said that in any event it was irrelevant whether I was or wasn't. A profound truth you learn after the first few firefights you're in is that it doesn't matter whether you're afraid provided you don't show fear and don't let it disable you. Indeed, fear turns out to be a highly useful stimulant that sharpens your senses and makes you better able to take care of yourself and your men. So it was no surprise to me that before turning in I checked all the windows, making sure they were properly latched, and locked and dead bolted the front door of the house and the door leading into the garden. Then I set the burglar alarm, including the motion detector. I looked forward to meeting the Voice, but I didn't want to be surprised. For good measure, I carried to my room the baseball bat that Harry kept next to the front door. Now was the time for sleep, but, although I was tired, sleep seemed beyond my reach. For some reason there was a Marine Corps first aid kit in the guest-room closet. I supposed I'd put it there at the time of my first visit to the Sag Harbor house after I got out of Walter Reed and forgot to take it back to the city. Some of the stuff it held had been given to me at Walter Reed and was a low-grade pusher's wet dream: Oxy-Contin, Percocet, Xanax, Tuinal, Ambien, and similar shit, tucked in with wound-packing and combat tourniquets. I needed an antianxiety pill like a hole in my head, but I did want to sleep and perchance not to dream. An Ambien went down the hatch.

The hateful stuff did its job. I woke up at seven the next morning feeling focused and mean. There were eggs, yogurt, English muffins, and orange juice that claimed to be fresh in the refrigerator, courtesy of Mary. Feeling starved, I made myself breakfast, skipping the coffee because I didn't know how to make the espresso machine work, and put on a clean sweat suit, a Harvard varsity tennis sweater, and a windbreaker, all of which I found in Harry's closet. Somehow I had remembered to bring my own running shoes and socks. Once dressed, I got the Audi out of the garage and headed for the Sagaponack beach. No cars were parked at the entrance, which was normal on a cold and cloudy Sunday morning. That was all right with me. I didn't want company, especially the usual dog owners. The tide was out, the sand was hard and smooth, I couldn't imagine better conditions for a run. Out of force of habit, I headed east. Halfway to Peter's Pond, however, that kind of unexplained perception that tells us, for instance, at a cocktail party that someone is staring at us made me aware I wasn't alone. Turning my head, I saw, heading in the same direction as I, a very big man— probably no taller than I but thicker and burlier—dressed in a silvery Lycra suit completed by a sort of mesh ski mask of the same color that hid his face. He was running very fast, and I didn't think he had reached his top speed. To test him, I increased mine. Instantly he followed suit. I wasn't sure how long I could sustain that rate and wondered whether it mattered, and what would happen if I turned around to face him. If his intentions were hostile, if he wasn't just fooling around, I thought I could teach him a thing or two about dirty fighting, however strong he was. I was spared the need to put the matter to the test by the appearance of a truck barreling toward us. Bonackers going home from crabbing in Georgica Pond, I said to myself and, dropping to one knee, waved it down energetically. It stopped, covering me with a shower of sand. I was having chest pains, I explained, and climbed into the cab. We drove off, leaving Bozo to his own devices. He had been running around us in circles and by way of farewell gave me the finger.

I showered and shaved quickly when I got home, dressed for the trip back to the city, and scooted over to the American Hotel for a quick brunch. Afterward I wrote a thank-you note to Sasha, threw my bag into the Audi, and, Harry's iPhone secure in my coat pocket, headed for the city. Harry had Sirius in the car pretuned to a station playing 1940s tunes. That was exactly what the doctor ordered. I'm like the B-19, loaded with Benzedrine. . . . I wanted to get my hands on the Voice's gizzard, perhaps his balls. Another part of my brain told me that the encounter with Bozo-on-the-Beach, which probably meant nothing beyond providing an insight into my unsteady nerves, was a useful reminder of the need to be watchful. My thoughts turned back to Kerry. It seemed to me even more likely that the psychopath who sent the Voice to kill Harry, because he believed that Harry had betrayed him or was going to betray him, would now go after Harry's most trusted lieutenant. Barbara Diamond being dead, Kerry was the principal repository of Harry's secrets. Barbara Diamond! Suddenly, I was really afraid and was glad I was alone in the car because I wasn't sure I could have concealed my fear. Was it possible that Barbara Diamond had been pushed under the subway train because someone thought she knew too much?

VIII

A note from Harry's—now my—housekeeper, Jeanette, greeted me at my apartment. I worked all Saturday packing, she wrote, so you can move to Fifth Avenue on Monday. I'll be in your apartment early on Monday to finish up.

Indeed, I could see that, except for the clothes I would need to have dinner with Kerry and first thing Monday morning, the closets were empty. My books were still on the shelves, but they, as well as the paintings and a few other odds and ends I wanted to take to Fifth Avenue that could not be easily transported by taxi, would be taken care of by the movers. The rest would be sold to whoever bought the apartment or given to the Salvation Army. So this was goodbye: a productive and happy period Harry had graced had come to a tragic and unnatural end. My laptop was on the desk in my study. I glanced at it longingly. Hidden inside it was as much as I had written of my new book. Somehow, its demands would have to be reconciled with the need to find the Voice and kill him.

It was too early to call Kerry unless I wanted to risk disturbing her while she worked with her team. I didn't. Instead, grateful that Jeanette hadn't packed or taken away the bottles I kept in the pantry, I made a stiff gin and tonic, carried it to my study, and let myself sink into my desk armchair. One gin and tonic called for another. I yielded to this evident logic, found an open can of cashews in the fridge, and returned to my armchair with the drink and the solid sustenance. Sipping much more slowly, I flipped through the mail Jeanette had left on my desk and found a hand-delivery envelope from Jones & Whetstone. In it was a letter from Hobson.

Dear Jack, he wrote, the partner I had thought might appropriately represent you in your capacity as executor of your uncle's estate is unavailable. I assume that in the circumstances you will retain a lawyer from another firm to advise you, and suggest that you ask him or her to contact me in order to arrange for the transmission of your file.

Interesting, I said to myself. Perhaps Kerry will understand what's going on, why no one can be found at J & W to replace legal-eagle Minot. She may even have ideas about some other trusts and estates lawyer I could turn to. Interesting also that Hobson chose to send this letter instead of emailing me. Why didn't he simply call me on the telephone? I think I understood the reason: the fop in him liked the idea of telling me to fuck off in a hand-delivered note. I put the letter on top of the dresser in the bedroom next to Harry's iPhone and was thinking of making a cup of coffee when my own phone rang. It was Scott.

I'm worried about you, he said. This stuff about being knee-deep in shit. It's not good for you.

Absolutely true, I said. At least the shit isn't of my making. Actually I was going to call you a little later this afternoon. I'm worried about Kerry's physical safety. I've thought about the obvious precautions—making sure that she double locks her door, asking who else has the keys to her apartment, warning her against wandering after dark down deserted streets, which is something she probably doesn't do anyway, but that's about it—I don't know what else to do. I thought you and your boys at Langley might have experience with this sort of problem.

After a pause, Scott asked, Just what kind of threat is this?

I wish I knew, I answered. It could be anything from someone breaking into her apartment to—far more likely—a fake mugging or a fake traffic accident, designed to hurt her, perhaps badly, or even to kill her. It could happen on her way to work or home from or to a meeting with a friend. Who knows? Mostly, I suppose, when she's alone. I might as well tell you, I've fallen for her and I think she's into me, so I hope to be with her most evenings. But you know how it is. People need space.

Right, Scott said. Congratulations! She's beautiful, and I like her. I suppose you'll explain the reasons for your anxiety on Tuesday, when you come here.

Yes, that's why I'm coming to see you.

Look, he continued, when someone the agency is involved with is under threat we provide security. A kind of super bodyguard. You can't organize anything approaching that, but that's the template. What people usually do when they feel apprehensive, or there has been a real threat, and for one reason or another they can't get police protection, is they hire a bodyguard.

He must have sensed that I wasn't buying this idea because he added, Yes, and a bodyguard doesn't need to be a muscle-bound gorilla with I'M A BODYGUARD stenciled on his forehead. There's someone I know who'd do, a retired FBI agent, inconspicuous, smart, quite able to handle an unpleasant situation if necessary, and one hundred percent honest. His real mission though would be to prevent Kerry's getting into such a situation. By keeping his eyes open and using his common sense. Of course, this guy's services aren't cheap.

Would it be possible, I asked, for this man to do his work without Kerry's knowing it? She thinks she's very tough. I can imagine her saying she doesn't want or need a nanny.

As I expected, Scott told me that such an unorthodox arrangement would make the bodyguard less effective. He'd ask Martin—that was the FBI man's name—whether he was available and would accept an assignment on those terms.

If you're really worried, he added, perhaps you should play bodyguard yourself until we work something out. I'll try to have an answer from Martin by tomorrow.

Not for the first time I thanked my lucky stars for having given me a friend like Scott. I knew he'd take a bullet for me, and I'd take one for him. That was how I'd felt about the men on my team and later in my Force Recon platoon. It was the one test that counted. I looked at my watch. Four-thirty. I had time for a badly needed nap before taking a bath and getting dressed for my date. But first I opened the locked file cabinet in my study. The top drawer held my arsenal: a tricked-out .45

and thirty rounds of ammo, my father's USMC Ka-Bar I'd kept on me through the Iraq and Afghanistan deployments, and a good-luck charm, the razor-sharp switchblade I took off the mullah I killed with my father's knife in Helmand, putting it right through his neck when I saw him start to pull the pin of a grenade. The asshole had come to the company HQ with a delegation of village elders who wanted to con the CO into releasing a Taliban we'd caught wearing U.S. infantry cammies, which was an offense punished by death. The pat down missed the grenade as well as the guy's switchblade. I picked up my weapons, examined them—it wouldn't be inaccurate to say that I caressed them—and decided to slip the switchblade into the side pocket of my jacket when I went to pick up Kerry. It might have been a different ball game with Bozo-on-the-Beach, assuming he really intended to get wise with me, if I'd had it in my windbreaker.

Kerry cried so bitterly that momentarily I regretted having told her the recording existed, even though the reasons for doing so remained as compelling as when I made the decision. Unless she understood what had happened to Harry she would not believe that she might be in danger. Anyway, it was done and could not be undone.

My attempts to console her were in vain. She shook her head when I offered to bring her another drink of bourbon on the rocks, a drink I'd discovered she liked, and pushed me away when I tried to put my arms around her. I felt lucky we'd made love before listening to Harry's iPhone. I don't think either of us would have been up to it with the Voice in our ears. As for me, I hadn't realized the urgency of my need for her until she opened the door and put her arms around me. Was this the hard-boiled litigator who could slice and dice a witness on cross-examination and who'd spent a day preparing for an upcoming courtroom battle? It seemed inconceivable. Her hair, her skin, were fresh and fragrant, her breath was sweet like a young child's, the body burning its way to mine through the layers of our clothes that of a young girl waiting for the boy to whom she'd decided to give herself.

Shush, Jack, she'd said, shush! and covered my mouth with her hand when she saw I was going to speak. Sag Harbor can wait. First come to bed. I won't let Harry and Sag Harbor take this evening away from us.

Afterward, when emptied and happy we lay quietly side by side, she asked about the hour of our dinner reservation.

Nine, I told her.

In that case, let's get dressed, have a drink, and talk.

It took her only a few minutes to get ready. I made her another bourbon on the rocks and poured one for myself. Then I ran through what Mary and Sasha had told me, gave her Harry's letter to read, saying that both Mary and I had been careful not to touch it with our bare fingers.

You were right. She nodded and asked to borrow my handkerchief.

I can't believe it, she said, and read it slowly once again, moving her lips as she did. But it's he, it's his tone of voice, only he seems to be mocking you. No, I can't believe it.

And have you noticed that he wrote it with a blue ballpoint pen?

Yes, she answered, and I never saw him use one. No, that's not right. Perhaps at his club, when he'd forgotten his pen and the waiter handed him one to use filling out the chit.

You've noticed he says he was expecting me to come back from Chile!

Yes, she said, it's incredible.

All right, I said, there is more, and it's worse. That is when I gave her Harry's phone. She got the voice-memo feature going with two taps of an impatient index finger. We listened and she cried and cried.

After a long while, she regained control of herself, washed her face in the bathroom, came back to the living room, and said, I need another drink. Please make it very strong.

We sat with our bourbons in silence until I put the question that I thought was first on the agenda. Could we get the police—or the FBI—to go after this guy?

Certainly not the FBI, she answered, anyway not on the basis of what we know at this time. The FBI concerns itself only with crimes that violate federal law. There doesn't seem to be any federal law involved here. Murders—this is almost surely a case of murder—are crimes under New York State law. Since the murder was committed in Suffolk County, I suppose it would be the Southampton police, perhaps with the help of state troopers—I really don't know how that works—who'd be in charge of the investigation, but perhaps there is a special unit in the county that would be brought in. The prosecutor would be the Suffolk County district attorney.

That is not what I had hoped to hear, I said.

I know, she answered, but your real problem is that we have only one real piece of evidence — the recording — that a crime has been committed. It's terrifying, but it doesn't even begin to identify a suspect. And given that Harry is dead and there is nobody who could prove that the recording is authentic, it's not at all clear that it could be introduced as evidence even if there were a trial at some point. The only thing we have, other than the killer's voice, is Harry's letter. It's a bizarre letter, you and I know it's not the kind of letter he would have written if he'd decided to kill himself, but it's his handwriting. You have to get the police investigators and the D.A. to think and feel their way into why this letter was indeed extorted, as the recording indicates, and what exactly it would prove at trial. So the question is, suppose you go to the Southampton police with the recording and the letter, where does this get us, and where do we go from there?

Nowhere, in my opinion, I said, not after you've put it that way. Not if it's the local police doing the investigation. You see what a great job they did when Mary called them. They didn't look for fingerprints or anything like that. They're dolts.

You may be too quick to judge them, she answered. There is a decent chance that they'd listen and open an investigation. Will they find this guy in Suffolk County? Unlikely. But perhaps there is a way of making this a statewide case.

Statewide case, I mocked. What makes us think he's in this state? How do we know where he came from? The answer has to be as I suspected. I'll have to find him, and I will find him, that much I can swear to you, but I don't believe it will be with the help of the Southampton or Suffolk County police. Anyway, let's go to dinner. I'm starved.

So am I, Kerry said, and this can't be a late evening. I have to be fresh and alert tomorrow morning. The argument is set for ten, and Judge Fiori runs a tight courtroom. All hell will break loose if we don't start on time.

I had decided not to mention Bozo-on-the-Beach to her, in part because I was coming to believe that the encounter meant nothing—how would the Voice and whoever sent him know that I was in Sag Harbor, and why would they want to attack me—and because, whether or not it meant something, I didn't want to spook her. But after the food and wine had done their work, and I thought both of us were more relaxed, I said, Kerry there is something I have to say that you probably won't like. I'm worried about you. You heard the Voice say that Harry was a traitor. Those lights going on and off through the house could have meant one thing only: the Voice was looking for documents. Presumably, he didn't find them. But if whoever it was who decided to murder Harry did it because of what he knew, and what he might betray, then aren't you at risk? You who were the closest to him?

She thought about it and said, It's crazy. Then she thought some more and said, Perhaps it isn't. What do you think I should do?

It's simple, I said. For openers, what is your schedule tomorrow?

My team—three of them—is picking me up. We're using a car service. We'll go down to court together.

And then?

After the argument, we'll go back to the office. The litigation bags weigh a ton, so we'll use a town car again, instead of the subway.

And tomorrow evening?

I walk home, take a long bath, and wait for you.

That's a perfect program, I said. Here is one refinement. I'll pick you up at the office and walk you home. Then while you take that bath I'll run an errand or two and will appear at your door at whatever hour you say. The rest of the evening I'll leave to your imagination, and it could include dinner out or a dinner I will have picked up when I'm running those errands.

Jack, she said, are you intending to be my nanny?

Yes, for a day or two, I said. Then I plan to be replaced by a professional. Kerry, don't protest, don't resist, I love you and I don't want you to be dead.

To my surprise, she didn't blow up. Instead, she took my hand and kissed it and told me she wanted to think.

I can't do it, she said finally. If we go to the police, months will pass before they find the monster. Or they won't find him. You say you'll find him and kill him. I know you'll try to, and perhaps you'll succeed. But that too will take time, especially as I'll do everything in my power to keep you from doing something stupid that will send you to a maximum-security prison for a good part of the rest of your life. So we're talking of having some guy or a team of rotating guys follow me around for months. I can't live like that. But I can promise you to be very careful about where I go and when, like late in the evening. There is no reason for Harry to have told you, but I'm a karate black belt, and I've done karate for years. I'm pretty good at it. I don't want to be dead either—I've just begun to be happy for reasons that have something to do with you—and you'll just have to trust me. By the way, she added, I've checked on Harry's papers. They're gone. Either dispersed among the client files to which they pertained— that is, of course, perfectly proper—or shredded. His email account has been wiped clean. That is in fact standard procedure. It's done four weeks after a partner's death. I'm so sorry, Jack!

It was my turn. I took her hand, kissed it, and thanked her for confirming what I assumed was the case. Hobson was a thorough bastard. There was no point in arguing about Martin. I could tell her mind was made up. When I saw Scott, he'd tell me whether the guy could do anything he considered useful without Kerry's knowing about him.

I hated to bring up more unpleasantness, but we had ordered coffee, and I wanted to get Hobson's letter out of the way. I handed it to her and asked, What do you think this is all about?

Whoa! she said. It's weird, but I think I understand. Harry was loved by his partners. The other T & E guys are straight arrows—one of them in fact is a woman I like a lot. Hobson could sell the shit about Harry to Minot; maybe he didn't even have to sell it, he just told him what to do. You've probably realized that Minot is an idiot. What you surely don't know is that his only trump card is that he's Hobson's brother-in-law. Hobson must have decided that once you told the J & W partner taking over from Minot the story about Harry's supposed dementia, the lost codicil, and so forth, in all likelihood the word would spread. The partners wouldn't buy it. And then all kinds of shit would hit the fan, to the great displeasure of Abner Brown.

I see, I said, and have you some lawyer you know I might go to?

After a moment during which she literally scratched her head, she cried out, I do, I do, my pal Moses Cohen, the super-Orthodox and superbright trusts and estates lawyer who has actually done a lot of litigation! After eight years as an associate at J & W he realized he was never going to become a partner, and four or five years ago he struck out on his own. He's doing very well, and he'll be thrilled to take you on. It'll be a good deal all around. He's a lot less expensive than J & W!

Goodness, I said. An Orthodox—super-Orthodox—trusts and estates lawyer? I didn't know that such a species existed. Kerry, this is a stupid question, but here it goes: are you by any chance Jewish?

You mean you've swallowed the Abner Brown shit I told you about? No, I'm not, though sometimes I wish I were. The Blacks—Schwartzes—came from Yorkshire in the mid-nineteenth century. My mother's family came from Ireland. My hair came from God.

I thank him for it, I said, and kissed the inside of her elbow. And do you think that Moses is up to squaring off against his super-Aryan former employers?

Nothing could give him greater pleasure, she answered, though I'm not sure it will come to that.

. . .

It's my turn, I said the next morning when Kerry's alarm clock rang at six-thirty. My turn to show you I'm a pro at squeezing oranges, making coffee, and cooking four-minute soft-boiled eggs. You take a shower and get dressed. She didn't protest. I was proud of her when she appeared at the breakfast table looking surprisingly rested—we'd made love twice after we went to bed so that in the end it wasn't an early evening—and every inch an ace lawyer ready for battle. I told her I was hoping to complete the move into the Fifth Avenue apartment by noon and asked whether she was free for lunch. She wasn't; it was the litigation partners' weekly lunch, and she'd be expected to report on the argument before Judge Fiori, but we'd see each other in the evening. As she'd said: she'd take a long bath and wait for me.

And I'll take you to a very good dinner, I said. Eight o'clock?

Earlier, if you like, she said. Seven-thirty?

I nodded and decided that this was as good a moment as any to ask whether she wouldn't like to move in with me. You'd see whether I'm a good roommate, I added. If I get on your nerves at any time, you can take a break from me over here.

Jack, she said, let's talk this evening. Of course, I want to live with you. There is nothing I want more. But I have a suspicion that the invitation is part of your Jack-the-nanny program. You want me in that building with doormen and elevator men, not to speak of Jack himself. Isn't that true?

She'd seen through me, and I wasn't going to lie.

That would be an added benefit, I answered.

I don't disagree, she said, but I assure you it's my habit to be careful, and from now on I'm going to be even more careful. Down to using the firm's car service if I go home after dark and asking the driver to stay at the curbside until I'm in the building. I know, I know, someone may be lurking in the building, and that is a risk. But there is another aspect to the situation: this is the wrong time for me to move to Fifth Avenue, even unofficially. Hobson's attitude toward you is hostile. It isn't likely to improve after you've retained Moses, and after you've taken whatever steps you're going to take to find the monster.

I call him the Voice, I interjected.

All right, the Voice. The point is that for the moment it is unwise for me, if I'm going to stay at Jones—and I've no other place to go—to become linked with you in the mind of Hobson. It's enough that every time he thinks of Harry I must pop into his mind as the lawyer who worked most closely with him. Let's not aggravate my case by linking me with you, Harry's nephew, heir, and champion, as your girlfriend.

What would you like to do about it, I asked.

Not much beyond not moving in with you just now. Avoid having lunch with you in restaurants where we'd be most likely to run into other J & W partners, take calls from you on my cell phone so my secretary won't necessarily know I'm speaking to you, attend the firm cocktail party next week alone, instead of asking you to be my date.

IX

The Law Office of Moses Cohen, Esq., was situated on Park Avenue, four blocks south of the offices of Jones & Whetstone, and was furnished in the same faux-minimalist style. Black-and-white photographs of old New York and Jerusalem hung on the walls. The latter, it must be said, were not to be seen at Jones. I called him from Kerry's apartment, and he agreed to see me that very morning. Moses, whom I had expected to be small and pudgy, turned out to be tall, with an athletic build and a handsome and open face. He wore a kippah fastened with a bobby pin to his full head of well-cut blond hair.

He heard me out—shaking his head in disbelief at the story of the codicil Minot had claimed to have forgotten or misfiled—and advised me not to answer Hobson's letter.

It's enough if I write to him stating that you've retained me, he said, and ask that he send over ASAP Harry's last will and testament, trust, and whatever else there is in his will file, everything relating to Minot's appointment as preliminary executor, as well as any papers they've submitted to get you qualified. I bet they've done next to nothing in that regard. You tell me they've shredded Harry's personal papers. That's cute. Once you become the executor you will have official standing. Depending on developments, and how much fighting spirit you have, we may want to commence a litigation to inquire into the shredding.

Although I was favorably impressed by Moses, I stopped short of telling him about Harry's having been pushed out of the firm or mentioning my belief that he had been murdered. It seemed better to let him operate, at least for the time being, unencumbered by that knowledge. Instead, I said I agreed with his plan of action and that Minot also had my own will, which Hobson or he should be asked to turn over to him together with Harry's file.

Do you have to have my existing will in your possession in order to prepare a new one? I asked. I'm really changing everything, so from my layman's point of view a codicil doesn't seem appropriate.

You're probably right about that, Moses said. Anyway, there's no need to wait for your existing will. Your new will, which I'll be happy to draft, will simply revoke all wills, codicils, and so forth. When we do get the old will we'll write on it "revoked," just as a matter of good housekeeping.

I'm relieved to hear this, I told him. My ideas are very simple. Do you think you could have such a document ready for me tomorrow, say by lunchtime, before I take the plane for D.C.?

According to Moses, nothing could be easier, a welcome

change from Minot who had taken three weeks and the assistance of an associate and a paralegal to produce my will.

That's great, I said. Here's the scheme.

I told him that I wanted to leave to Jeanette an amount equal to that which Harry had bequeathed to her in his will, the copyright to my first book to Yale, the copyright to my second to my prep school, to Mary an amount to be increased by taking into account the number of years she would have worked for me prior to my death, to Scott such items of my personal property as my executor might select, and to Kerry the balance of all I had, real estate included. I wished her to be my executor.

Moses nodded, a gesture that I thought was intended to express admiration. Does Kerry know about this?

No, I said, she doesn't. Nor do I want her to know it at this point. The fact is that I love her and want to marry her as soon as she'll have me. My health is excellent, but I engage in some dangerous pursuits and can't help realizing that I may not live to see that happy day. If something happens to me, I want her to be almost as well off as she would be if she were already my wife.

Understood, Moses said. I think I should get a rough idea of your assets, as well as, of course, the correct titles of your books.

It was clear he hadn't read them. Most likely he hadn't been aware of their existence. I forgave him and went over what I owned.

Moses nodded again. Kerry is a lucky lady, he said, I hope you do get married and live very happily ever after. If you stop by tomorrow at noon, your will shall be awaiting your review and, if you approve, your signature.

I thanked him, and went to "my" Fifth Avenue apartment.

Jeanette had a sandwich and a salad ready for me and shook her head disapprovingly when I declined the offer of seconds. I've got to work, I told her. That was the truth. I'd just arranged to give away copyrights to two works. The third one was waiting to be created and copyrighted in its turn. You'd think that it would be impossible, or at any rate extremely difficult, to pick up the thread of a book if you've been under as much stress as I and were subject to as many interruptions. Luckily, writing is a magic activity. Once a book is anchored in its placenta, wherever that is located, it remains viable, because all the while, whether he's conscious of it or not, the story that the writer wants to tell never stops maturing. His characters surround him and clamor for his attention. Minutes after I had opened my computer I was typing away. By the time I stopped in order to get ready for dinner with Kerry, I had more than fulfilled my usual quota. Fourteen hundred twenty-two words. I read over what I had written, revised it, and gave the text another reading. It wasn't half bad.

As a student, I'd been accustomed to relying almost entirely on my memory, to the point of not taking notes in class or on what I'd read, or making outlines before writing a term paper. I'd get the structure of an essay fixed in my mind and plunge in. Making checklists compulsively was different—a habit I formed at OCS. Speak to Sgt. A about X;

have men review procedures B and C; verify ammo counts. Those lists held anxiety at bay. No wonder, therefore, that when the shuttle to D.C. was delayed, and the plane, with passengers on board, was held first at the gate and then on the runway, I pulled out of my computer case one of Harry's legal pads and began to tick off tasks completed and those demanding attention.

Dinner with Kerry had hardly been a task. I didn't write it down on the pad. I luxuriated in the memory. She had told me of her courtroom triumph: before the conclusion of the hearing, the judge had as much as ruled from the bench in favor of her motion, congratulating her on the persuasiveness of her presentation. His opinion would be issued before the end of the week.

The client is thrilled, she said. If the judge comes through it will be a real shot in the arm; my position in the firm will be one hundred percent stronger. Hobson would have to be nuts, which he may be, considering what he did to Harry, to fuck with someone who's doing work that Western really appreciates. Western Industries doesn't bring in as much in billings as Brown, but it's in that league.

That was good, even if—but she didn't know it—Hobson's machinations could no longer imperil her ability to support her parents or pay off her student loans. My visit to Moses didn't make the checklist either, but it had been everything I'd hoped for. He had drafted my will in clear language and gotten the bequests exactly right. There was something to be said for note taking by lawyers as well as by combat infantry squad and platoon leaders. Moses had scribbled every time I opened my mouth. We were all set. So long as I was alive,

I'd make sure Kerry and her parents lacked for nothing. And she'd be well provided for if I disappeared.

Now came the hard part. I wanted Scott in my corner because of the steadfastness of our friendship and his loyalty and because I valued his brains and experience. There was also the agency connection, from which I expected miracles, against my better judgment. At the same time, I recognized that I didn't have a clear idea of what I could expect from him, what the miracles might be. Help from his colleagues at the agency and perhaps at the FBI? A way to involve the agency officially? The meagerness of my own experience— when you came right down to it, I had none—and the difficulty of the task I'd set for myself, to find the Voice and kill him, were disheartening. And beyond lay a task of even-greater difficulty: finding and punishing whoever had sent him. The plane finally lifted off. I shrugged my shoulders and started the checklist:

1. Identify the Voice's accent.
2. Are there fingerprints other than Harry's, Mary's, Kerry's, or mine on Harry's letter or the envelope?
3. Sweep the house in Sag Harbor for fingerprints and DNA.
4. Harry's clothes and the rope are in Suffolk County police custody—get hold of them (how?) and subject them to a similar sweep?
5. The Voice's question in answer to Harry's about who had sent him—think about who'd want you dead. How to go from there to validating my suspicion that it was Abner Brown who'd wanted Harry and

perhaps Barbara Diamond dead and had sent the Voice to kill them?

6. Why was Minot hell-bent on getting hold of Harry's papers? Answer: Hobson told him to do it. Was Hobson following Brown's orders? If he was, did he know Brown's reasons? If they weren't Brown's orders, what was Hobson's reason?

I stopped, not knowing what the next step should be, and told myself that what I'd been able to figure out didn't amount to a pile of beans. Since I was through as a Marine Infantry officer, perhaps I had better stick to writing books. How low would I sink in Scott's estimation once he'd heard me out? I'd find out soon. The die was cast. I paid for a bourbon on the rocks, drank it, and fell asleep.

Scott had told me to go to Alexandria directly from National Airport. He'd be waiting for me at home. Where he lived, a flounder house, turned out to be an architectural gem. As soon as I'd washed up, he gave me a tour, pointing out the original paneling, cabinets, and floors, all of which he had lovingly restored. When we sat down for drinks, he looked at his watch and said that since the dinner reservation was for nine we could talk without feeling rushed and continue once we got to the restaurant. He'd chosen it because it was very quiet.

After I'd given him a summary of the events and the conclusions I'd drawn, he asked for the iPhone and Harry's letter. I gave him both.

Let's see if I can enhance the sound, Scott said after we'd begun to listen, and connected the phone to a device on his desk.

Suddenly, the voices were loud, multiplying the horror.

You poor bastard, said Scott. I hate to think of you listening to this alone. I think you're right. The guy is very likely from the Balkans. We have specialists in recognition of accents and speech patterns at the agency. There's a man like that on my team. He's a regular Professor Higgins. I'll get him to zero in on it.

I don't know whether you realize, he continued, that there are criminal gangs crawling over the Balkans like lice. Real dregs of society: career criminals and thousands of demobilized soldiers who'd learned during the war not just to kill but to rape and torture. Every kind of crime against humanity. Those gangs are equal-opportunity employers. You'll find Christians and Muslims, Serbs, Bosniaks, Croats, Montenegrins. They're not interested in internecine wars. It's only about money, nothing else. There's even a mostly Kosovar gang, an offshoot of KLA—the former Kosovo Liberation Army—a terrorist organization if there ever was one that had managed to pull the wool over many people's eyes. All those bums are in the same businesses: drugs, principally Afghanistan-sourced heroin transiting through Turkey into the Balkans, arms, trafficking in women and children, yes, children sold into slavery, money laundering, and fielding hit men. They've spread into Central and Western Europe, and they're beginning to be seriously active in Latin America and lately the U.S.

Why do you know so much about them? I asked.

They're something I'm looking at, he told me, because of current terrorist links and even greater terrorist potential. It ties in with my work in Afghanistan. We'll get this fellow's national origin narrowed down, and we'll search our database for likely candidates. You know: a hit man, probably early middle age, probably physically imposing, speaks English, works for an outfit that would be hired by a high-class employer. That last factor may be key. If I accept for the time being your Brown hypothesis, his bosses have to be of a type that people working for Brown would trust with a delicate job. Don't get your hopes up, though. If something turns up it will probably be pure serendipity.

What about my idea of a fingerprint and DNA sweep? I asked.

That's easy and will be done. I have friends with the right skills who wouldn't mind moonlighting over a weekend in Sag Harbor—for instance, if you graciously lend the house to a small group recommended by me. Since it's your house, and you give permission, there are no legal complications. We don't need to go before a judge for a search warrant! The one thing I must ask you almost goes without saying: not a word about that to anyone. We're not supposed to ply our trade at home. Let's set this up when I visit you this coming weekend. By the way, will Kerry be there?

I said I hoped so.

From my selfish point of view, I couldn't ask for better, but please be careful. The more she gets involved, the more she will be exposed.

But Scott, she is involved. She couldn't be more involved. There is no one who knows more about Harry's work. Putting that aside, I love her, she loves me, and I want to marry her. With you as my best man!

That was the first time I'd said out loud that she loved me. Of course, to whom except Scott, and perhaps Jeanette, could I have said it?

Congratulations, old friend! I very much want to be your best man, so I want you both to stay alive. Now listen to me, Scott continued. That you are having an affair, that you're in love—all right, it's a given. Try to be discreet about it. The next point is more important. Don't ask me how I know it or why, but I do know that somehow knowledge attracts danger. Especially in a case like this. Already she knows too much. So think carefully about how much you tell her of what you discover, and when.

I nodded and said I understood.

Good! By the way, I've talked to my pal Martin Sweeney, the retired FBI agent, about protecting someone who doesn't want to be protected. He says it's awkward, but it can be done. Essentially, it's no different from putting a discreet tail on someone, and he'd be willing to do it. What do you think? I have a feeling it would be money well spent, even though, thank God, the chances of our ever finding out whether he was useful are close to zero. Why don't you have a cup of coffee with him? You'll see what kind of impression he makes on you.

That struck me as a sensible idea, and we agreed that I'd call Martin as soon as I returned to the city.

That letter, he continued. Your uncle had extraordinary presence of mind. Thinking up and including in the letter so many signals to put you on the alert. We'll get it analyzed as well. You never know what leads the right kind of microscope and trained eyes can discover. By the way, I was struck by the mention of the family Bible. Was your uncle particularly religious?

Good God no! I replied. He went to church occasionally—if he happened to like the minister. And we don't have a family Bible! It was another way to make sure I got the point. Like saying I'd been in Chile where I hadn't gone, the weird expressions he never used, the Mark Twain quotation, writing with a blue-ink ballpoint pen when he detested blue ink and ball-point pens.

So cool under fire, Scott mused, and yet, when he was on that ladder, he didn't jump on top of the Voice and take his chances instead of putting the noose around his own neck. He was himself a big and heavy man. How do you explain it?

I'm not sure, I answered. I've been mulling over that question. It could be that the Voice was really huge and strong looking, and Harry realized that he wouldn't manage to hurt him. Instead he'd be badly hurt himself. Don't forget the beatings the Voice administered. There's a kind of despair that sometimes overcomes people in a fight when they know they can't win. They want it to be over—the sooner the better. He may have also thought that the Voice would hurt the cat very badly, and he didn't want that. You don't have a dog or a cat so probably you can't appreciate Harry's love for his cat. It's not an exaggeration to say that Harry would have risked death—hell, would have died—to save Plato. Take an obvious case: the house is on fire. Do you doubt that Harry would have plunged into the smoke and the flames in order to save his cat? Or it may have been a form of disgust. He felt he'd had it. He didn't want to tangle with the Voice, he didn't want to face the obvious fact that someone—almost certainly Abner Brown—hated him enough to send the Voice to kill him; he preferred in the end to let the Voice get on with his job.

There was another explanation, which was shameful; I couldn't keep it entirely out of my mind. That yellow streak of Harry's my father and grandfather had suspected. He should have gone for it, but his nerve failed. I didn't want to share that suspicion with anyone, not even Scott.

Very strange, Scott continued. Too bad, I suppose.

And the Brown connection, do you think it's there?

That's a very difficult question, Scott answered. Let's have dinner. We'll talk while we eat.

As it turned out, however, we spoke first about Scott's life. I knew that shortly before our expedition to Patagonia he'd broken with a woman who worked in the policy-planning group at the State Department. They had been together for more than a year. It was her idea, and he told me then that he didn't understand the reason. He was sure that he loved her. It had seemed to him that they were getting along just fine, they had the same tastes, they knew many of the same people. She too had been at Yale, three or four years behind him. She refused to tell him why. However, a couple of weeks ago, he ran into her at a party in Georgetown. She was with a man who also worked at the agency, a Russian affairs specialist, whom he had always considered a friend. He was able to observe them for some minutes before they became aware of his presence. It was painful, he said, they couldn't keep their hands off each other. She had never been that way with him. It wasn't a large party, and eventually there was no escaping an exchange of the usual greetings and getting into a conversation.

We're grown-ups, right? he said. I run into this guy at meetings, in the elevator, in the cafeteria. So I had to act civilized and detached. Only the entire time they talked they acted so guilty, really so shitty, that they confirmed what my intuition had told me as soon as I saw them. They'd been having an affair while she was still with me. A petty betrayal, the sort of thing that I guess happens all the time, but it left me feeling sour and misanthropic. The perfect mood for Mr. Abner Brown and his enterprises. Let's see what you've got on him.

What I had, according to Scott, came down to this. First, it was clear that Harry had been murdered. Second, there was Kerry's account of Harry's having discovered a pattern of lawbreaking when he prepared for a possible stock exchange listing of some of Brown's companies, and the fact that Brown, presumably realizing what Harry had found out and what his likely response would be, turned on Harry and asked the chairman of Jones & Whetstone to remove him from work on his companies — after all those years of Harry's having been his friend and privy counselor. Finally, the very fact that the Voice was a hired killer, and his crack about someone who wanted Harry dead. That last point isn't a figment of your imagination. It's right there in the recording.

Hit men are used when drug dealers and other professional criminals settle their accounts, but otherwise? I'm assuming that Harry wasn't involved with drugs and didn't have big unpaid gambling debts.

Of course he didn't, I replied.

So the hit man would have to be sent on account of some other connection with a big-time criminal activity. Isn't that about it? Doesn't your case, if you want to call it that, rest squarely on the proposition that Abner Brown is a big-time criminal who didn't want to be exposed? he asked.

I nodded.

As for the lies Hobson told about Harry's supposed dementia, Scott continued, and his and Minot's attempt to get hold of Harry's personal papers, that's probably craziness relating to law firm politics. How do you get rid of a respected, perhaps beloved, senior partner who hasn't done anything wrong that you can point to? Could Hobson have said it's because an important client says I don't want him handling my matters and I want him out of your firm? Perhaps you have to invent a reason. How he got Harry to agree to leave is something else. It may be that we'll never know. The personal papers are a tougher problem. Could Brown have said first I don't want Harry Dana on my matters, and then, after Harry has committed suicide—let's call it that for this purpose—could he have called Hobson with another request? Please make sure there isn't anything derogatory about me or my affairs in Harry's personal files. I wouldn't want such material to come into the hands of persons who aren't bound by a professional obligation of confidentiality? Otherwise, you'd have to posit that Hobson is aware of the illegality that Harry found and is participating in a cover-up. That may be going too far.

I don't disagree, I murmured, but don't forget Barbara Diamond.

I'm not, Scott said. But as you perhaps don't know or have forgotten, each year a lot of people, in the hundreds, are killed in New York City by subway trains. Some jump under the train as it approaches, some are pushed, some fall off the platforms in what seem to be accidents, and on and on. You have the coincidence of timing, and a very plausible premise that if someone wanted to kill Harry because of what he knew he might want to kill Barbara as well, and would want to kill her as soon after Harry's death as possible. But to get with these shards to Abner Brown—I don't know how you do it unless you learn more about what it is that Harry discovered. Kerry may be able to help. Of course, if we could find a lead to the Voice or his bosses . . .

Sure, we can talk to Kerry, I replied. But I doubt she knows anything beyond what she's already told me. Frankly, I don't know how you're going to get to the Voice except through Abner. Searching your database with nothing to go on other than his accent and speech patterns makes looking for a needle in a haystack seem easy.

Something may turn up, Scott said. We spend a lot of time studying the flows of goods in violation of sanctions, especially the Iran and North Korea sanctions, and the flows of money. They're like mighty rivers. And a good number of Brown businesses, Abner's companies, just happen to be on riverbanks. Exactly what is the business of those companies? Apparently it involves nothing that needs to be disclosed to any government, certainly not the government of the U.S., because no disclosure has been made. So that's one aspect of Brown's enterprises. How good is the internal system of compliance? Have these enterprises been investigated? Not really. There have been problems with the EPA, but the proceedings have gone nowhere. That may be related to Brown's political power as well as the EPA being generally fucked up. You'd be shocked if you knew how many congressmen and senators are in effect on Abner's payroll. Perhaps you wouldn't be, not if you follow carefully certain investigative reporters. You'd be horrified to learn how his fingers extend into high reaches of the Justice Department and how many higher-ups in the FBI and, yes, in the agency have bought into his political shit. Or are under his sway for other reasons. So we foot soldiers must tread very carefully. But all the same, I'm going to give some thought to how what Kerry calls pervasive illegality both abroad and here might intersect with our interests.

What Scott said about Brown's potential ability to have his way with our government brought me up short when he suggested that I leave Harry's iPhone and letter for further expert study—especially of the phone's content—and safekeeping. He would give me a couple of CDs and Xerox copies of the letter to take back to New York.

After your experts have finished, would you place the phone and the letter in some locked cabinet or safe in your office? I asked. Quite frankly, I'm worried about your not being able to prevent someone who's a Brown ally, for lack of a better word, from removing them.

I don't think we're quite there at the agency. Scott laughed.

But don't worry, that is not what I had in mind. I was going to place them in the safe I rent at the Wells Fargo branch I use here in Alexandria. If you trust me you will be able to look on them as an insurance policy against at least some of the dangers you are likely to be courting.

I got back to Manhattan the following afternoon. Kerry had gone to Boston for a meeting with a new client, referred by Western Industries, and was coming back on Friday, on the seven o'clock shuttle. We'd agreed that I'd pick her up at the Marine Terminal. She'd have everything she needed for the country with her, and we would drive out to Sag Harbor without stopping off at her apartment. That gave me two full days for work on my book and two other pieces of business. The first I accomplished as soon as I got home. It left me breathless with excitement, and I decided that for the time being I wouldn't discuss it with anyone, not even Kerry or Scott. The second was straightforward: I called Martin, the FBI man. He was free and agreed to come for a drink at the apartment later that afternoon.

He turned out to be a conspicuously inconspicuous man of middle height and solid build. Under a black down parka, which I hung up in the hall closet, he wore a navy-blue blazer with brass buttons, a blue oxford-cloth Brooks Brothers button-down shirt, a striped navy-blue-and-red necktie, and gray flannels. The brown boots with reinforced toes were the only item that wasn't part of the Ivy League middle-management uniform. The kick they delivered, I surmised, could be lethal.

You realize that what I'll be doing isn't foolproof, he told me. Security work never is, and the young lady's not knowing that she's being protected and not cooperating is a complication. But I'll keep an eye on her from when she leaves her apartment until she calls it a day. It will help if you tell me in advance as much as you know about her schedule. That way, if I know she's planning to stay at her office except when she goes out to lunch—that's just an example—I'll know I can take a couple of hours off. I understand that we don't know the nature of the threat or what sort of person I should be looking out for.

We don't, I answered, except that we do know that my uncle was murdered by someone who appears to be a professional killer capable of considerable personal violence. Using his hands, and not just a weapon. Someone who speaks English fluently, with some sort of Slavic accent, and makes mistakes. The danger would come from that source, from whoever sent the killer. But there is no reason to think that if Kerry is attacked it will necessarily be by the same man. It could be anybody.

Righto, Martin replied. I'll plan to start on Monday. Without indiscretion, will the young lady be spending that night here or at her place? Let me know when you find out. We'll do our best and keep in touch. If I don't answer the phone you may want to send me a text message. Sometimes you're in a situation where it's awkward to talk.

I worked steadily into the evening, ate the cold supper Jeanette had set out for me, and went back to my desk for another couple of hours. The next morning at five I left the building for my first real run of the week. The weather being raw, with no improvement predicted before the weekend, I slipped on my Nike windbreaker. The switchblade fit comfortably in the pouch pocket. I'd put it in the overnight bag I checked going to D.C. and coming back—otherwise, it had been my constant companion. I crossed Central Park at Seventy-Ninth Street and ran north on the West Drive as far as the North Woods before turning east toward the Harlem Meer. For someone who hadn't exercised seriously for a number of days and had been staying up late and drinking more than usual, I wasn't in bad shape. I ran effortlessly and fast, leaving behind the few other benighted souls who had ventured out in the early morning dark and the cold. By the time I had left the Meer and was heading south a feeling came over me that partook of irrational exultation and the sort of aura that sometimes saves lives on patrol. I fancied that I was no longer alone, that steadily gaining on me was a runner whose silhouette and togs and gray ski mask were intimately familiar. Bozo-on-the-Beach! I cried out. Aha, this time I'll get you. I'll run faster—there's no limit to my reserves of strength—but, Bozo, I know you'll catch up with me, and in another minute you'll be on top of me. But just before that happens, I suddenly face you and drop into a crouch, the open knife in my hand. Inertia propels you with such force that you fly over me and crash headfirst on the asphalt. I stomp you, and when you stagger to your feet I cut you!

A group of three runners, two men and a woman, running north came into view, putting an end to my hallucination or waking nightmare. I continued south on the East Drive, left the Park at Seventy-Ninth Street, and jogged home.

Soaking under a hot shower, I reviewed the bidding. If Bozo had really followed me into the park, what would I have done? This time I would have certainly stood my ground, the knife tipping the scales in my favor. Would I have killed him? Not unless he revealed himself to be the Voice, the likelihood of which I now doubted. The Voice was a pro. If sent by Brown—or whoever had sent him to murder Harry—he'd have dispatched me on that Sagaponack beach with the same relentless efficiency. It wasn't conceivable that Brown would tolerate Bozo's kind of bumbling. Then who was Bozo, and what was the explanation for his pursuit of me on the beach? This was another question to which, at least for the moment, I didn't have an answer. He could be just a jerk looking for a fight. Why not? Most of the world's population are weirdos.

Some things had become clearer to me. I resolved that if I found the Voice or, more likely, if he found me, I would try, whatever violence it took, to make him spit out the name of his client and the truth about Barbara. Had he murdered her as well as Harry? And I now knew that in order to accomplish this and kill the Voice—in self-defense, ha! ha! ha!—I couldn't let my friends' zeal for justice get in the way of my vengeance.

This last thought requires a word of explanation.

On the shuttle back to New York I mulled over my conversations with Scott and was struck by the inanity of the answer I gave when he asked whether Harry had been religious. He went to church if he liked the minister, I had said, and we don't have a family Bible! As soon as I got home, I rushed into Harry's library. It's true that we Danas do not have a "family Bible," or anyway a Bible that any of us, and certainly not Harry, would have been pretentious enough to describe as such. That was—I now understood—yet another of his pathetic brave attempts to get my attention. But he did own a Bible, and it wasn't some beaten-up paperback. I remembered having seen in his library a Bible with an exceptionally fine leather binding, which he told me had belonged to his and my father's grandfather, Ezekiel Dana, the founder and for more than thirty years rector of an Episcopal boarding school in southern Massachusetts. And there it was, in the place I remembered, next to a fine edition of the complete works of Dickens. Seek and ye shall find. I turned the pages until I got to the Gospel according to Saint Matthew. And inside it, at chapter 7, I found carefully folded sheets of legal-pad paper. At the top of the first sheet he had written: Every good tree bringeth forth good fruit, but a corrupt tree bringeth forth evil fruit. Matthew again—consistent with the hiding place. The rest of that sheet, as well as the second, were given over to two intricately drawn diagrams that in fact resembled trees. The roots of the first spread wide under the ground, and its branches reached toward the sky, while the second, which on close inspection I realized was the mirror image of the first, had been planted upside down, its branches buried, its roots aloft. Linked to the branches by dotted lines were handwritten notes. More handwritten text consisting of numbered paragraphs followed. It was Harry's handwriting, meticulous and legible. Perusing the notes and the text I recognized the names of well-known companies and individuals—businessmen and politicians—both American and foreign, as well as citation to laws. At the bottom of the second page appeared an aphorism

I couldn't identify, possibly one that Harry had invented: Each thing has its double and each such double is corrupt. Was that another clue or Harry's judgment on Abner Brown's enterprises or perhaps both?

Kerry would have the knowledge and skill to decipher and interpret these pages. If they were, as I fully expected, a Rosetta stone that unlocked Abner Brown's and his companies' crimes, my darling former assistant U.S. attorney would be champing at the bit to turn them over to the government for prosecution. That was what I too wished, so that Harry's message, of which he had made me the bearer, would dismantle Brown's operation and put him behind bars. But I would be able to settle my accounts with the Voice only if I succeeded in goading Abner Brown into sending him to kill me, and that was something he would do only if he thought I had to be silenced. The corollary was that if Abner learned that I had already let Uncle Harry's cat out of the bag—I squirmed at the expression but couldn't get it out of my head—he would no longer think that siccing the Voice on me was in his interest, and he was far too smart, I was sure, to do it merely out of spite. Yes, I had to goad him into sending the Voice because on my own I would never find him. Then, once I had him before me, I would kill him. Or he would kill me, a possibility I couldn't dismiss. The grander goal—bringing Abner Brown and his business to account—would be the work of others, whether I lived or died, and would be accomplished if the incompetence, pusillanimity, and corruption of public officials did not thwart it.

X

The telephone rang the next morning just as I settled down to work. I looked at the identification window on the receiver, saw the Jones & Whetstone number, and pressed TALK. A no-nonsense female voice inquired whether she was speaking to me. Reassured by me that such was the case, it said, Please hold for Mr. Lathrop. In a moment, I heard his patrician accents.

Oh Jack, he said, you may not remember me but I'm one of your poor uncle Harry's oldest and best friends. The name is Lathrop, Simon Lathrop. Harry was one year ahead of me at college and law school, and we'd been together ever since at Jones. I had the pleasure of attending the book party Harry gave in honor of your first book, and you were kind enough to inscribe it for me. Jennie—that's my wife—and I are heartbroken over what happened, and you would have heard from me sooner if I hadn't been in rehab at Burke until ten days ago. Would you by any chance be free to lunch with me today?

I assured him that I knew perfectly who he was and remembered meeting him, and was free, whereupon he asked me to meet him at his club. It was the club to which Harry had also belonged, and I had lunched and dined with him there frequently.

Simon, as he asked me to call him when we shook hands, met me in a small room on the ground floor behind the hall porter's desk, and suggested we take the elevator to the dining room.

It's these wretched things, he said, waving one of his two Canadian crutches. They make climbing stairs pure hell.

Having offered me his condolences again as soon as we sat down at table, and expressed his shock and sorrow, he explained that he had been away from the office since the week before the party for my second book. The artificial hip that he had received five years earlier had started to disintegrate, causing a great deal of trouble. He had tried to postpone the procedure to replace it so as not to miss the celebration, but it turned out there was no flexibility in his surgeon's schedule. It had to be then or two weeks after Christmas, and he had been unable to wait that long. The discomfort was too intense.

He had jogged my memory.

I remember now, I told him. Harry mentioned the operation. Apropos of your not being there, something that struck me then, and seems more significant now in retrospect given everything that has happened, is that only one J & W partner attended that party. Quite a few had come to the one for my first book.

Really, Simon observed, that is very odd.

At the time I thought that the guest list had been trimmed because the publishing house was the host, I told him. Now I'm not so sure.

Really, he said once again, and went on to relate that the operation to replace the malfunctioning artificial joint turned out to be a much bigger deal than he had expected, and the rehabilitation surprisingly difficult, considering his physical condition before the operation, which, except for the hip, had been quite good. Harry visited him at the hospital twice and said nothing about having problems at the firm. Then, during one of the subsequent visits at the rehabilitation center in Westchester, Harry astonished him by announcing that he had decided to retire, in large measure because he would no longer be doing Brown work.

When I tried to talk him out of it, Simon continued, one of the arguments I used was that difficulties with a client can sometimes be smoothed over, particularly if the client is a fellow like Brown, who makes up his own mind, with whom one has been on terms of personal friendship. You can have a long talk and find your way out of the difficulty. But he made it so clear that he wasn't interested in a reconciliation, and that he was in fact delighted to end a relationship that had become an albatross, that I began to think that I was coming through as naïve. He said he was grateful that it was over. Otherwise, he would have never made up his mind to stop working, not until the retirement plan forced him out, and he'd come to realize that getting out was what he'd been yearning to do. He'd be able to read, to go back to his piano, to travel, and to play Cupid. And that is, of course, where you come in, dear fellow.

Simon paused and looked at me as though he expected me to offer a specific rejoinder. Not understanding what he was driving at, I said nothing.

Come, come. Simon chuckled. It's not that hard to guess what he meant. I agree it was an out-of-character thing for Harry to say. I had to chuckle then too, because my wife, Jennie, and I tried to play Cupid with him once or twice—not before the Inca came on the stage, because way back then he was always involved with one glamorous lady or another—but after the calamity, when he was at first so grief-stricken and later so lonely. I pleaded with him to let us introduce him to some really wonderful women, but all to no avail. And there at Burke, at the rehab, he told me he was going to make sure that you and a certain young lady he thought the world of would get together. He went so far as to say that he looked forward to playing grandfather as the sequel to playing Cupid.

It was my turn to laugh.

I'm beginning to think I know whom Harry had in mind, I replied. If I'm right, the arrow didn't miss the target.

Kerry? he asked.

I nodded.

He'd be so happy, Simon said, one wishes one could believe he knows it. That is one of the reasons why I find his having committed suicide—less than two weeks after I last saw him—so utterly strange. If it hadn't happened one would have said it was the last thing he'd do. There is another troubling element. I've been told by a partner who works for me on some of my matters that the reason for Harry's withdrawal from the firm, and apparently also for having been asked to stop working on Brown matters, is that he was suffering from dementia. That is something I really can't accept. I had long and far-ranging conversations with him during the period of my convalescence. We talked about the past, about current firm issues, about politics, and even about our investments—about life and death, if you like—and there isn't an iota of doubt in my mind that Harry's intellectual acuity and emotional balance were unimpaired. His intelligence was as always absolutely of the highest order!

I nodded again, and told him that I had spoken to his doctor, who at his recommendation had become also my doctor. He told me conclusively that Harry had had his annual physical examination two weeks before Christmas, and he could confirm that he was in excellent health. There were no neurological problems, and certainly no symptoms of anything like dementia.

Incredible, Mr. Lathrop said. Have you any explanation for what happened?

None for what happened at the firm, I answered. Will Hobson told me when I saw him upon returning from Brazil that Harry showed symptoms of dementia, which had been detected by Abner Brown, and gave that as the reason for Harry's being removed at Brown's request from work on Brown matters, as well as for having been asked by him, Hobson, to take early retirement. The dementia part of the story would seem to be an invention.

A rotten lie, Mr. Lathrop interjected.

I don't object to that word, I said, in fact I'll adopt it. Neither you, nor Harry's doctor, nor other people close to Harry who were in contact with him shortly before he died believe any such thing. I don't know why Mr. Hobson chose to lie to me and spread the lie in the firm.

I can perhaps think of a reason, Mr. Lathrop replied.

I'd like to hear it.

And the suicide, how do you explain it?

I found myself liking and trusting this fine old man, and remembered that Harry had indeed spoken of him as his best friend. All the same, I took the instant decision not to tell him I was convinced that he had been murdered, or that I had what I and Kerry and Scott all thought was conclusive proof that a crime had been committed. My reluctance was akin to not wanting too many cooks in the kitchen. I didn't know yet how I was going to find the Voice, or how I was going to kill him, and having this grand old lawyer begin to think that he was somehow part of the team, and perhaps had to take responsibility for what I would do, could only complicate the task.

So, feeling somewhat ashamed of myself, and hoping I didn't show it, I said that I had not come to terms either with the fact of the suicide itself or the manner in which it had been done. But could he tell me, I asked, the reason he had thought of for Mr. Hobson's actions?

It's a strange business, he told me, law firm jealousies. Jones & Whetstone is one of the few remaining great law firms that still adhere to the lockstep system of compensation for partners. Are you familiar with that concept?

I nodded.

Well, then you know that how many billable hours you rack up or how much business you bring in isn't reflected in your compensation. It's all based on seniority, unless, of course, a partner really screws up, which, I'm happy to say, hasn't happened more than a few times in the firm's history. In that case, the management committee may cut his or her compensation for a year or two, sometimes as a prelude to a forced departure. I'm telling you all this to set the stage. Harry and Will Hobson were taken into the firm in the same year. Therefore, their earnings as partners have been identical. However, even though Will is an excellent lawyer, with a tough analytic mind, the difference in productivity and contributions to the firm has been huge—and glaring. Will has made his contribution to the firm, and it's not negligible, as a competent, no, in fact a remarkably effective bureaucrat. From the beginning, he has been on every committee, he has been the moving force behind every so-called strategic-planning initiative, and on and on and on. Stuff that Harry and I have always basically considered a waste of time. What he has never had, however, is the one thing that makes the firm live, which is the ability to attract and hold clients. I don't believe that Will has ever had one significant client of his own. He has only worked on matters brought to the firm by other partners, those who have their own clients, and among those Harry has always stood out. To put it simply, clients had been always drawn to Harry as though to a magnet, and he had always done brilliant work for them, all the while leaving the firm's administrative bureaucratic tasks to the likes of Hobson. I am of the opinion that Hobson has never been able to forgive Harry for that, or for Harry's generosity in bringing him, Hobson, into Brown matters. Because there they were in the real world, where Harry was number one, and Hobson, the firm leader, was figuratively speaking carrying his briefcase. And don't think for a moment that the contrast between those two or between their relative value to the firm was lost on the older partners! Or, I would guess, on Abner Brown!

How extraordinary! I said.

Poor Harry meant well, and he had such good character that I don't think he allowed himself to be aware of Will's resentment. Or Will's pent-up ambition. What I'm driving at, as you've probably figured out, is that it is not impossible that Will placed a banana peel in exactly the right place for Harry to slip on in the Brown relationship. Or that he seized on something Harry had done or said and made sure that it enraged Abner Brown. Obviously, I can't tell you what Hobson has done, but I have no doubt that he had a hand in engineering Harry's fall. Having done that, he would have wanted him out of the firm, and I suspect that Harry was so disgusted by what he saw had been done that he couldn't wait to get out the door. Then Hobson spread this vicious rumor to cover up his tracks.

How horrible, I said, to trip Harry up if that is what he did. But why the lie? Why the rumor?

Because if it had been said that Harry was leaving because Brown no longer wanted him to work on his matters, that he'd rather have Hobson on them, partners would have protested and pleaded with Harry to stay. His value to the firm was so great. More dangerous yet, they might have wanted to know just what he had done that was wrong. But if they were told, Look, fellows, he's losing his mind, or He's already as good as lost it, don't embarrass him by talking to him about it, just let him go in peace . . . Well, that's another ball game.

I see, I said, struck by the similarities in Simon's and Scott's analyses.

Yes, and it's my fault, Simon continued, or rather the fault of my goddamn hip. If I had been at the office instead of the hospital, Harry would have talked to me and I would have taken steps—I have a certain weight in the firm—to undo the harm with Brown, but the chances of that initiative's success would have been less than fifty percent, and certainly to put an end to the nonsense of quitting the firm over whatever Brown and Hobson had cooked up. And there would have been no slander campaign, no lies about dementia.

I wish, indeed, you had been there. You've given me a great deal to think about, and a great deal to regret.

We'll stay in touch, he told me. Jennie and I would like to have you and Kerry over to dinner. By the way, don't you worry about Kerry's standing or future at the firm. Since Harry treated her like a daughter you may assume that Hobson hates her, but her reputation at J & W is solid gold and, just in case, she has me to cover her back. I've had this bum hip, but otherwise I'm in fine shape, and I'll be at the firm for a good while still, perhaps longer than Hobson. I have no problem with your telling her that.

I thought a great deal during the weekend with Kerry and Scott about the conversation with Simon Lathrop, my gratitude growing for the explanation he'd advanced for the role that office dynamics might have played in the catastrophe that overcame Harry. I thought it would be of great value in the confrontation with Abner Brown that appeared to be the necessary next step. But I was more than ever convinced that I had been right not to draw him into my plans, and I continued to think that the decision to withhold from Kerry and Scott knowledge of the discovery I had made in the Gospel according to Saint Matthew was sound. It was necessary, however, to put those sheets bearing Harry's message in a safe place that Brown's minions would not discover in case my mission failed and the Voice or another of Brown's thugs killed me. That was an absolute necessity. I had another wish, which may appear frivolous to a reader who is not a writer. It was to finish my third book. I thought that if I worked hard, and with total concentration, I could have a publishable draft in my agent's hands within three weeks. In four weeks, therefore, I would seek out Abner Brown in his Houston lair. Just how I would get him to receive me I hadn't figured out yet. It occurred to me that I might seek Simon Lathrop's advice.

The three-week pause would be useful as well in ways that had nothing to do with literature. Scott's forensic team would be arriving in Sag Harbor the following weekend. They would scour the house, and would use their wiles to borrow—Scott's expression—Harry's clothes and the hemp rope for examination in the Langley laboratory. The work on relating the Voice to the database was still in progress, Scott's linguist friends having confirmed that almost certainly the Voice was a Bosniak Serb. Most probably one of the swine involved in the ethnic cleansing in Bosnia. A number of subjects fitting that description were known to be active in gangs whose operations had been detected in the U.S. A narrowing-down process had been started, designed to determine who among them was known or suspected to be actually present in the country, and if possible his connections. There's no use looking for the address, Scott laughed. They're one hundred percent illegal, moving in the underground, which may include luxurious hotel suites and safe houses, inhabited by drug dealers, money launderers, and hit men.

A remark Scott let fall fascinated me. If we find some connection between Brown and money laundering it may develop into a connection to terrorist organizations. Even the beginning of that sort of proof, and the agency and the FBI will be after him with everything they've got. And, believe me, they won't let go.

That proof, I now realized, might well be lodged on the sheets of legal pad paper tucked away in my safe.

XI

finished book number three on time. It was a disguised retelling of my love affair with Felicity and her ditching me after I'd gone to war, which at the time I'd considered callous and cruel. As I wrote my novel, my point of view changed and became fairer. I came to understand that she had been opposed to the war and considered it foolish, and that for her I was not some *chevalier sans peur et sans reproche* responding to the call of his suzerain but a self-important jerk who'd never stopped to consider her point of view or the future we had hoped to have together. I didn't agree with her assessment of my attitude, but there it was. It couldn't be swept aside. Harry would have understood my new book better than anybody. That was too bad. There I was in his apartment, working in the study he had furnished for me with such care, and I would never again knock on the library door, hear his voice tell me to come in, and hand him my manuscript as he half rose from his favorite leather club chair to greet me. Kerry knew no more about Felicity than that such a woman had existed in my life, and I didn't think I had the time, if I was going to keep to my schedule, to tell her enough to prepare her to accept the new book. If my agent and my editor thought it was publishable, she would read it later. When the time came. This was not the moment when I should trouble her. But I did email the manuscript to Scott. He called me two days later and said he'd stayed up both nights reading it. He thought it was the best thing I'd done, even better than my war book. I thanked him profusely and sincerely, but wished he'd skipped the comparison. Authors, I was discovering, are like parents: they resent having their progeny compared and ranked. All the same, Scott's praise gave me the encouragement I needed. I printed my text and sent it to my agent, and realized I was now free to turn my attention to the Voice. The plan to ask Simon Lathrop how he thought I should go about getting to see Abner Brown still seemed good. Kerry and I had been to dinner with him and his wife, and I had no doubt about his friendship or willingness to help.

He invited me once again to lunch at his club and greeted me with a big smile saying, Look, Ma! No crutches. He'd walked to the club from the office, he went on to tell me, the hip behaving just fine, and suggested that we climb the two flights of stairs to the dining room and leave the elevator to the geriatric set. In fact, he'd had an idea. After lunch, we'd trot over to the law firm together. His office was on the same floor as Hobson's, his in the northeastern corner and Hobson's in the northwestern. We'd have a cup of coffee, and he'd make sure that Hobson was au courant. It would be fun to fire a shot across his bow. Was I game?

I said that naturally I'd be delighted.

Excellent, excellent, he returned, and set about writing out our lunch order.

As soon as he had finished, I laid out the problem. I wanted to see Abner Brown at his office or in whatever other setting Simon considered advisable, and I wanted him to be alone. No lawyers or PR types or other advisers present. What was the best way to avoid a brush-off?

What's the purpose of your visit? Simon asked. That's the first question Brown or whoever you get through to will ask.

My answer would be that I need to understand what happened to Harry, I replied. I'd go on to say that he had been in excellent health, and had no problems or serious worries of any sort other than the disappointment he must have felt when you, Abner Brown, asked that after all those years of working together he have no further involvement in your or your companies' affairs. Based on your long knowledge of Harry, was that a sufficient reason for him to hang himself? I also want to know, I'd say to him, whether it is true, as William Hobson claims, that you dismissed Harry because you'd come to the conclusion that he had become demented. There are some other related issues I'd like to discuss. And that's pretty much all I'd want to tell him on the telephone, I continued, if you think I should call him, or in a letter if you think I should write. I think I need to keep a card or two up my sleeve.

Such as what? Simon asked.

For instance, the way Hobson's acolyte Minot pulled a fast one to get himself appointed preliminary executor—if that's the correct term—and disregarding the codicil that named

me executor, went through Harry's safe at home and at the
bank and rifled through his papers at home and in Sag Harbor, and the way that all of Harry's personal papers at the firm
have disappeared, shredded. I'd like to ask Brown whether
that was done at his behest and, if it was, for what reason.

I wasn't aware of this—I don't know what else to call
it—hanky-panky, Simon said very slowly. And what is being
done about the administration of Harry's estate? Is Minot
handling it? Presumably he had Harry's will in the firm bank
vault.

After I explained that it was Moses Cohen, Simon told me
that I had done the right thing. Minot's conduct struck him
as unprofessional. Then, after a pause, he said, Let's eat our
salad. I'm deeply upset by this story, not only on your and
Harry's account but also because it reflects so badly on the
law firm where I have spent my entire professional life and
to which I'm devoted. As you can imagine, I'm not going to
pretend that this hasn't happened or that I don't know about
it. Now do eat your lunch.

We ate in gloomy silence.

When we finished, Simon said, Your plan is good. I don't
think I can improve it. When we get to the office, I'll give you
Abner Brown's direct office number. Access to it is strictly
restricted by his people, and I've only had it since the time
he made his successful push to buy a seat on the museum's
board of directors. The chairman and I were deputized to
negotiate with him, and we did squeeze out the largest sum
any donor has contributed in the museum's history. Were we
right to take his money if it meant putting his name on a wing
and his person on our board? Neither the chairman nor I is

completely sure of that. Anyway, your call will certainly be answered, possibly by him personally. Or if not by him then by someone who will get the message to him right away. If it's one of his assistants, stick to the line that you are Harry Dana's nephew and need urgently to speak to him. The reason? Your reasons are of a nature that you do not feel free to discuss with anyone other than Mr. Brown himself.

Simon's plan to have my visit to his office at the firm be the first skirmish in the war with Will Hobson miscarried. The enemy was in Texas, expected to return the next day.

At least we know that, said Simon. Don't call Brown before Hobson has cleared out of Houston. I'm going to learn more about the sordid behavior you've described and take appropriate action. Here is the magic telephone number. You've got my home and cell numbers?

I nodded.

All right. Good luck to you, and let's keep each other posted.

On my way home from Simon's office I stopped at a Third Avenue RadioShack with the intention of buying a burner to use when I made my call to Abner Brown's office. As I waited for a salesman to help me, I decided against the purchase. There was a greater chance, it seemed to me on reflection, of Brown deciding not to answer if he saw a number and no name when his phone rang than if he saw my name. I would derive no advantage from masking my identity.

Kerry and I had an early dinner that evening at her place, and got up correspondingly early. She was catching a shuttle for Boston. I remained in the apartment, put away the breakfast dishes, and made the bed. Eight o'clock in New York City. Seven in Houston. I'd read somewhere that Brown was one of those five-in-the-morning-at-the-office freaks. If the report was true, it wasn't impossible that he was there alone, and would handle his own calls. Unless, of course, he didn't answer and let the caller leave a message. I dialed the number, using my regular cell phone. There was a longer than usual pause, and then two, three, four rings and I heard a man's voice say: Brown here. What the hell do you want? He spoke with an ever so slight Texas accent that I was ready to bet a thousand dollars was affected. The son of a bitch had been to Groton, Princeton, and the Harvard Business School. The family ranch was adjacent to the King Ranch, and I was willing to believe that he'd spent parts of summer vacations there, playing cowboy. But the family also had a spread in Maine. It would be a miracle if whatever Southern intonation he had when he moved on from grade school had not disappeared, only to be replaced with this phony lilt that went with his lizard-skin boots and whatever other rich Texan oilman and rancher paraphernalia he sported.

I want to see you about my uncle Harry, I answered.

What the fuck for? was the retort. He's dead. No use beating a dead horse.

Why he died, and how, aren't dead issues. I have questions about them that only you can answer, and I need to have them answered.

Then write me a letter.

No, I replied, there are things you know and things I know that can only be discussed face-to-face. I'm ready to come to

Houston, and I don't need more than two hours of your time. And I want to see you alone.

Give me your number, he said. My secretary will call you and give you the date.

With that he hung up.

This is the soft-landing brush-off, I said to myself. Don't call me, my secretary will call you. I'll never hear from the bastard and will have to think of some other way to blast my way in. Perhaps Simon will have an idea. But I was wrong. At nine-fifteen my cell phone rang. Brown Enterprises. Aha! His secretary came in at eight. Accent like pecan pie.

Captain Dana? she inquired, simpering.

Speaking.

This is Mr. Abner Brown's assistant Eileen, Captain. Mr. Brown will be glad to receive you next Wednesday at two p.m. at his office in the Brown Tower. Do you have the address? If you let me have your email, I'll send it to you together with all other directions.

I thanked her and gave her my email address, whereupon she asked whether I would like to send her my flight information, in which case it would be a pleasure to have me picked up at the airport. She'd also be glad to make the hotel reservation.

You're too kind, I said, thinking that perhaps it was better to keep my itinerary to myself even though Brown Enterprises surely had ways to get at that sort of information. That won't be necessary. I don't know how long I'll stay, and I'm pretty good at dealing with Mr. Hertz and Mr. Avis.

All right, she replied, it would have been a pleasure, Captain, I'm sure. If you change your mind, just let me know. May

I add one word for myself? I'm so very sorry, everybody here at Brown is so sorry about your uncle Mr. Dana. Such a lovely gentleman!

That gave me a week to take an important precaution. Stuff happens. It was fair to assume that from the moment I left Abner Brown's office no company in full possession of the facts would write a policy on my life. It was my duty, therefore, to make sure that, if the Voice or another Brown minion got me before I got them, the Rosetta stone to Brown's misdeeds must find its way into Kerry's and Scott's hands. How much Simon Lathrop should be told, and when, seemed to me to be separate issues that could be dealt with later. I didn't think the Rosetta stone should remain in the safe at my apartment. Presumably Jeanette wouldn't stand on legalistic ceremony with Kerry, and would allow her access to the safe if something happened to me without waiting for her to qualify as my executor—the memory of Minot's maneuvers was fresh in my mind—but there was no telling what other factors could block that simple solution, such as the police sealing the apartment. Perhaps that wasn't something that was likely to happen. I didn't know, and didn't want to take the time to find out. The best solution that occurred to me was to rent a safe-deposit box at the Madison and Eightieth branch of my bank, with Kerry, Scott, and me having access to it, and place Harry's sheets in it. I decided against making copies. Where would I hide them, and for what purpose?

Scott was coming to the city on Thursday night, staying

with his mother. I would invite him and Kerry to lunch at the apartment on Friday, and we'd go over to the bank afterward so they could sign in as persons with access to the box. Would I tell them the nature of the document we were putting in the box? My inclination was not to do so. They would realize that by pursuing my plan I would put my life in danger and—Kerry especially—would try hard to talk me out of it, arguing that if the Rosetta stone worked we should immediately proceed against Brown as the principal villain without taking grave and unnecessary risks. I recognized the force of that line of reasoning but so far as I was concerned it broke down when it came to the Voice. Whatever we had on Brown might well be sufficient, after lengthy trials and appeals, to send him up the river, but would it, even in combination with the iPhone and Harry's letter, identify and get the Voice? The risk that it wouldn't was big, and it was the one risk I would not take. On the other hand, Kerry and Scott were too intelligent and too concerned about me to agree to become joint custodians of a document without knowing its nature. I decided on a compromise. I'd tell them I thought I had found Harry's indictment of Brown and his business and that I wanted their solemn promise not to read it or remove it from the bank except with my permission or if something happened that took me out of the picture. Until the last moment I wasn't sure that they'd agree. In the end they did, and I was left feeling relatively comfortable that they'd keep their word.

To go back to that afternoon, however, I found a message from Kerry when I checked my emails. Her meeting was on the right track. She thought she'd catch the seven o'clock shuttle back. Could we have a dinner plus a sleepover? A wave of such happiness overcame me that I let out a whoop.

Come directly to Fifth Avenue, I answered. Dinner and even better will be waiting.

Then I called Simon and reported that I had wangled an appointment. He wanted to hear all about it, and I gave him an account with the expletives intact.

I'd like to be there with you next week, he told me, and not particularly as a fly on the wall. I'd like to be there as Harry's oldest and closest friend. But it may be best that you speak to him alone. But I haven't been inactive either. A group of us seniors have met and we've come to the conclusion that the circumstances of Harry's forced retirement from the firm were not in accordance with the firm's governance or traditions. Hobson had acted against the firm's interest. We intend to give him an opportunity to present his case. Unless he mounts a surprisingly strong defense he'll be asked to step down as chairman. Perhaps he'll be asked to leave the firm. I don't suppose I need to ask you, Jack, to hold this in strictest confidence—from everyone, including Kerry. The younger partners haven't been brought in.

Of course, I said, but I too have a request. Please do nothing until I return from Houston. And please stop your group from doing anything as well. Abner Brown would doubtless learn of any steps taken with regard to Hobson. Perhaps Hobson would tell him, to seek his support. I would really hate it if my visit to Brown were thrown off the track by what was going on at the firm.

A point well taken, Simon replied. You have my promise.

That done, I met with Martin the bodyguard at a Starbucks, told him over a latte when Kerry was getting back from Boston, and went on to say that in my opinion she'd be at increased risk beginning next Wednesday.

I'm going to do something aggressive with regard to the man I think was the employer of the thug who murdered my uncle. I'm going to tell him, I said, that I know my uncle had been murdered, that I have proof of it, and that I have a very clear idea it was he who'd sent the killer. Lastly, I'll say I'm going to go ahead with all sorts of revelations unless he sends the killer to get rid of me. Sends him to me so I can kill him.

Gutsy thing to do, Martin replied shaking his head, I'm not sure I'd recommend it, but that's your call. If you're right about the employer and the whole setup, the young lady will for sure be in greater danger. I'll take appropriate precautions. One suggestion: please ask her to stay out of the subway. If she's going anywhere other than from her apartment to her office and back, please ask her to call this car service.

He handed me a card. Printed on it was the name Safe and Sound Limousines followed by a cell-phone number.

This isn't a car service, Martin continued. It's my partner, Lee, another retired special agent who will drive her and relieve me as needed. And please ask her to order in, instead of going shopping, and pay in advance by credit card, tip included. That way she can tell the delivery man, unless she knows him, to leave the order outside the door. I know she'll object, but you can say it's just for a few days. She does know what you're up to, doesn't she? She'll understand this is good advice.

.   .   .

There was a small cube of a room off the lobby at the Brown Tower where you passed security before taking the direct elevator to Abner Brown's office. It reminded me of the room that served the same purpose at our embassy in Kabul. A body scanner booth, shelves divided into pigeon-holes for storing equipment such as cell phones you weren't allowed to take inside, three blond young men indistinguishable from one another in Brown Security overalls who looked as though they'd been to Iraq and made it home. I'd left my cell phone in my overnight bag in a locker at the airport, having foreseen the need to check it before going up to see Brown, and having no desire to have its contents inspected. After the scanner there was an expert pat down. Not for a weapon, because any such thing would have been picked up by the scanner, but—I hadn't a doubt—for a wire.

What's this? one of the trio asked, fishing out of my coat pocket the CD case.

A CD case with a CD in it, I answered.

All right, leave it here. You can pick it up on your way out.

Won't work, I said, it's a CD I'm bringing for your boss.

One of his colleagues took the case from him, removed the CD, and passed it through what I assumed was some sort of explosives detector, said, It's OK, put the CD back in the box, and shoved it toward me. I replaced it in my pocket.

Good to go, he said into his walkie-talkie, and pushed a button that opened the elevator door.

Eileen, even more honey sweet than on the telephone, greeted me in the anteroom in which the elevator deposited me, and said Abner would see me right away. Would I like a cup of coffee or another beverage?

Coffee, I said, if you please, no milk and no sugar.

All right, she cooed and spoke into a gold-colored receiver, Captain Dana's here for you, Abner.

A growling noise replied. She smiled and told me to follow her.

I'd Googled him and found a variety of images—taken from the sites of the Metropolitan Museum and the hospitals and public library in New York City on the boards of which he sat—and was prepared for the pudgy bland face, the domed bald pate, and the rimless glasses. His small stature surprised me when he rose behind his desk and waved to a chair across from him. He didn't hold out his hand for me to shake. I sat down and said, Thank you for receiving me.

A pointless visit, so let's make it short, he answered.

I would have liked him to go on in this vein, but he was interrupted by a ping that announced the arrival of Eileen and a waiter carrying a tall glass of iced tea, which he set in front of Brown, and my coffee. I glanced at the door through which they—and previously Eileen and I—had entered, and noticed that it was padded. Probably a good idea, I said to myself, giving Brown's outbursts and language, and perhaps there were other reasons as well.

You said you had reasons, Brown continued. Let's hear them.

I recited the speech I'd rehearsed for Simon Lathrop.

You're wasting my time, Brown replied. I don't know why

the fuck Harry Dana hanged himself. It's a stupid-ass idea to ask me. As for me telling Hobson that Harry was demented, that's pure bullshit.

Then why did you tell Hobson that you didn't want my uncle to do your work anymore?

It's none of your business, but I don't mind telling you. Your uncle was a fine lawyer so long as he stuck to lawyering. His problem was he got too big for his britches. He was telling me what to do, instead of doing what I told him to do and what I paid him for. And I paid a lot. So I told him to keep his fucking nose out of things that he wasn't hired to take care of and it turned out that he couldn't understand that simple instruction. Instead, he had the balls to come here in my plane and give me a lecture on my behavior! Said he'd take measures—that's the expression he dared to use—if I didn't do this and that and that! He was fucking going to blackmail me! Let me tell you, young man, nobody does that. That's when I told him to get out of my office and turn over all the work he was doing for me to Will Hobson and whoever in his firm Hobson designated.

I see, I replied. And for good measure you had Harry killed.

Brown rose. There was on his desk one of the Italian Renaissance bronzes Kerry had admired, a Hermes standing on one foot, his other foot, also shod in a winged sandal, raised in the classical pose. The messenger god on his way, to do Zeus's or Hera's bidding. Brown seized him by the foot he had set on the ground and advanced toward me.

Easy, I said, put that nice statuette down. I'll break your arm if you come near me.

Brown retreated a few steps but held on to the bronze, determined, I supposed, not to lose face. But that is exactly what I wanted him to lose, so I said, I'm going to count to three. Either you put Hermes down or I'll take him from you. And don't even think of pressing any buttons. I'll kill you with my two hands before any of your goons get through the door. One, I counted, two . . .

He put the bronze back on the desk.

Good, I said, I note that you haven't denied that you had Harry murdered.

Of course I deny it, he answered slowly, you're raving.

No, I'm not, I told him, I've got a couple of things for you to look at that will change your tune. First, here is a copy of the letter Harry wrote and left in an envelope addressed to me on the desk in the room where he was found hanging. Read it. You knew Harry very well. You tell me whether this was a suicide note he wrote voluntarily or one that he was forced to write.

I put the sheet on the desk before him. He picked it up and I could see by the movement of his eyes actually read it.

So what the fuck? he replied. It reads like a letter written by a fucking queer. I always thought he was one. How am I supposed to know what kind of suicide letter he'd write?

I've been told you're very smart and I thought you'd use your imagination and your judgment. But never mind. I've got something for you that's more direct and easier to understand. I see you've got quite a sound system here.

I motioned toward the Bang & Olufsen stereo components installed on the bookshelves.

Here is a CD, I continued and handed it to him, of the murder scene, the scene during which Harry was forced to hang himself. It was recorded on Harry's iPhone, which the murderer you sent failed to notice. Go ahead, put it on. You'll find it's good listening. Instructive.

As though in a trance, Brown inserted the disk into the player, pushed the right buttons. The Voice filled the room.

Brown had listened standing up, leaning against the bookshelf. He shook his head afterward, walked briskly toward his desk, and sat down.

What do you want? he said. This recording doesn't prove I sent this guy. You have no proof. Why don't you get into your Hertz car, drive to the airport like a good boy, take the plane back to New York, and hope that nothing unpleasant happens to you? Got it?

I laughed. He had genuinely amused me.

It's in your interest to make sure that nothing untoward happens to me. If it did, the original of this recording, right on Harry's iPhone, and the original of the letter, and more information besides, would be placed in the hands of prosecutors. There is nothing you or I could do to stop it. You see, whether or not I have proof, I'm convinced that this Croat or Serbian thug was sent by you, and I'm also convinced that you arranged the murder of Harry's secretary, Barbara Diamond. There is no end to the evil in you, Brown.

Cut the fucking bullshit, Dana, he replied.

I was glad to see that a little color showed on his face.

It's not bullshit, I said, it's the truth and it has consequences. You see, Harry left behind something even more interesting than his letter. He left a detailed map of your crimes—your crimes and the crimes of your businesses. It's the crimes he stuck his nose into, right? It's because he figured out exactly what you were up to that you wanted him out of your affairs, it's because of the discovery of your companies' pervasive and systemic corruption and illegality that you had him and Barbara killed. Isn't that exactly right?

This is bullshit too, he replied, and you're taking way too much of my time. Once again, what do you want?

I want you to send this guy to me. Send him to kill me, because I'm going to kill him instead, and that is what I want. I want to kill him. I want to watch him die. And you better be quick. There are only so many days before I release the stuff I have to the government.

It was Brown's turn to laugh. And laugh he did—hysterically. You want me to admit to you that I had anything to do with your uncle's death? You want me to concede that I know the meathead on the recording, and you want me to send Slobo to you? . . . Dana, I'm not an idiot, and apparently you're a hell of a lot dumber than you look. If I were you, I'd be damn careful from now on. And the same goes for whatever other motherfuckers you've roped into your crazy little plot against me. You may be a war hero, but you're in way over your head on this one and you've left me with only one option.

XII

He'd said his name! He'd actually said it! He knows that the Voice is called Slobo.

So it was war now, a condition with which I am thoroughly familiar. And I'll confess that it's one with which I am thoroughly comfortable. If you're going to kill your enemy and survive, you need training, meticulous attention to detail, and luck. The training I'd received in the Corps is the best in the world, and I know how to keep my eye on the ball. I'd been lucky during successive dangerous deployments, the kind of wounds I'd received being par for the course. Would my luck hold? I figured I was about to find out.

My Hertz Lexus was in the Brown parking lot. I approached it carefully, dropped down to one knee, and inspected the undercarriage. Nothing out of the ordinary there. I'd pasted a strip of Scotch tape across the right-hand corner of the trunk cover before heading for the Brown Tower. It hadn't been disturbed. No one had monkeyed with the trunk. The Lexus was equipped with new technology that allows you to unlock the car's doors and start the motor from as far away as twenty or twenty-five feet. I looked around. There was no one nearby I'd be putting in danger. I took the electronic key out of my pocket, pressed the open and ignition buttons, and took cover behind an SUV. Just in case. I guess Brown wasn't in that much of a hurry or he didn't want to have to explain a murder in his parking lot. There was no explosion. I drove to the airport, got rid of the car, and took the shuttle bus to the AA terminal. There was a flight for Washington, D.C., leaving a few minutes before the scheduled departure of my JFK flight. I had plenty of time. I switched my reservation, got a new boarding pass, and, not being sure whether Brown, who surely knew my cell-phone number, could tap into it, found a pay phone. First I called Scott, told him I was coming to D.C., and asked whether I could see him and spend the night at his house. The answer to both questions was yes. Next I called Kerry, on her Black-Berry as she had recommended. She was in a meeting and, when I asked whether I could call back, said she'd be free in fifteen minutes. I took advantage of that time to call Martin, the bodyguard.

I had the meeting with the employer, I told him, and I delivered the message almost exactly as I said I would. He heard me out and said, in slightly different words, you're dead, and so is everyone else you've gotten involved in this bullshit.

Martin gave a long whistle. Were you wired when you talked? he asked.

I didn't even try, I told him, I knew his security wouldn't let me get away with it.

Right, he interjected, that was a stupid question but I sure wish you had been.

Anyway, I continued, we both know this is bad news for Kerry. You should consider yourself on high alert.

Right, said Martin again, and I'll put my partner Lee on high alert too. It would be a great help if the young lady accepted our presence and cooperated. If you can get her to do that, she should call me on my cell phone. I'll take it from there and make the necessary arrangements.

Exactly what I think, I told him. I'll be speaking to her in a few minutes.

Kerry was in her office when I got her, waiting for my call. I told her I was going through D.C. to see Scott and wouldn't get to the city until tomorrow and gave her the highlights of the conversation with Brown.

He's really something, she said. What a slip of the tongue!

Or maybe he doesn't give a shit, I replied. Anyway, he's vicious and dangerous. I owe you an apology: when you said you didn't want a bodyguard, I pretended to let the subject drop. In reality there is this guy—a very capable and civilized former FBI man—who has been shadowing you. I take Brown's threat very seriously, and I really want you to cooperate with this guy—his name is Martin Sweeney—and his partner, Lee. Please call Martin and work things out with him so that you are as safe as possible with the least interference in your daily routine and so forth. This is an absolute necessity. They thought nothing of killing Barbara, and they'll think nothing of murdering you.

She protested but only feebly, and we made a dinner and sleepover date for the evening of my return. At her house.

. . .

What can I do to help? asked Scott, in addition to giving this guy's name to my boys, which I'm doing right now.

He was busy tapping on his cell phone.

Send a drone! I replied and held out my glass for a refill of bourbon.

You talk as though this were some kind of big joke, he complained, but I'm dead serious. A Predator is just what is called for, but we don't use them stateside.

The time will come, I laughed, all too soon. . . . Quite seriously, I have been giving thought to how they'll go about getting rid of me. Somehow I don't believe that they'll go for a straightforward assassination. It would provoke the most energetic police reaction. And I don't think they'll try to have me commit suicide. It would be hard to get people to believe it runs in the family. So I think it's most likely that this guy will be told to make whatever happens to me look like an accident. I don't see how they'd stage it at my place on Fifth Avenue or even at Kerry's, where I'm happy to report I'm spending tomorrow night.

Is Martin on the job? Scott interrupted.

Yes, I said, and she's playing along—at least for now. So, to go back to the accident, an obvious choice is to have me hit by a car or a motorbike running a red light or jumping on the sidewalk. That sort of thing happens all the time, and in many cases the hit-and-run driver manages to disappear even if it's a real accident. Right or wrong, that doesn't worry me. The subway is something else, but I hardly ever take the subway and won't do so until this is over. Of course, the range of possibilities increases exponentially if they plain want to kill me. You have the possibility of a gangland-style shooting by someone walking behind me in the street or from a parked car or when I'm running in the park. The guy could also use a knife. I'll be careful.

Scott nodded.

Pursuing the idea of an accident, I tend to think that a sadistic bastard like Slobo wouldn't mind returning to the scene of an earlier triumph. In that case, wouldn't he want to do the deed in the Sag Harbor house, and wouldn't he want to do it in a way that will give him time to play with me? That takes me to the question of timing. Logically, Brown should want to have me killed tonight or tomorrow, the sooner the better, to minimize the chances that I'll go public with whatever it is I have. But it's got to be done right. If you accept my Sag Harbor hypothesis, since I'm not going out there this weekend, but am going the weekend after, I think that is when Slobo and I have a date.

You aren't taking Kerry, are you?

I shook my head.

Then let me come with you. This doesn't have to be some sort of duel.

I'd love to have you, I said, but he'd realize you're there and decide it's no longer a solo job, particularly if it's supposed to be an accident. You'd spook him. There is another thing. To tell you the truth, I want to do it alone.

Scott's pager, or whatever device it was, beeped and he went into the kitchen.

That was the office, he said. Hot off the press. It may just be that we know your Slobo. The first name, Slobo, is the usual nickname for Slobodan. The profile, to the extent that we can extrapolate, points to one Slobodan Milić. Born in 1975, Bosniak Serb, fought in one of Karadžić's units, a gangster and killer on Interpol's wanted list. How he slipped in on a tourist visa in 2008 is for the moment a mystery—one I'll try to elucidate. Another example of the State Department's and Homeland Security's prowess. Of course, there is no record of his leaving, which in itself means nothing, or of his whereabouts. But all this will be looked into right away. We do have his fingerprints, but in Sag Harbor the son of a bitch must have worn gloves and was goddamn careful. As you know there was nothing in the house, nothing on the rope, nothing on your uncle's clothes, nothing on the shears that cut the poor cat's whiskers. And we do have his mug shot, which will be coming here over the wire. That I think is helpful. As soon as I have it I'll email it to Martin. Is he working with Lee?

I nodded.

That's another good man. I think knowing what the guy looks like makes their job easier provided that they don't start assuming—and you shouldn't start assuming either—that Brown will necessarily use Slobo. Don't forget that Slobo made a big mistake by not checking thoroughly for any sort of recording device. He may be in big trouble.

I nodded again.

We also have his weight, one hundred ninety pounds, and height, six foot one. Shorter than you but more solid. And don't forget that anyone who fought with Karadžić has had a lot of on-the-job training. Not like yours, but still nothing to take lightly.

Thanks, I said. I wonder whether Slobo's and my paths

haven't crossed already. We can talk about that over dinner—
if dinner is on the program.

It is, said Scott, and now let's get to the core of the problem. You're my best friend, probably my only real friend. So
I'm not going to pull an agency stunt on you and grab whatever that paper is that we put in the safe. I could, and perhaps
I even have a duty to do it, because if I read you right it's a
fucking guide to Brown's illegal businesses. I've been looking at his activities, and if what you've told me about your
uncle is accurate, and if my hunch is right, those activities
probably affect the security of the U.S. Why should you then
delay turning the document over and delay our getting on his
tail? And why should you, along the way, expose yourself to
mortal danger when you have everything to live for? Kerry.
Your new book. You can make your own list.

I remained silent for a while before answering. These are
the reasons, I said finally. First, I want to kill that bastard.
You know that, and you and I know chances are that he'll get
away while you're cranking up your apparatus. Not because
you want to be slow, but because bureaucracies are slow. Second, even if the feds or whoever catch Slobo, he'll get off
with a prison term. That isn't acceptable to me. Third, there
is the problem of Brown's influence. You've mentioned the
senators and God knows who else he has in his pocket. Suppose he derails the pursuit? What then? That's why I want to
go first. If a couple of weeks pass and nothing happens, you
can have Harry's document, or you and Kerry can have it, and
you can do whatever is most efficient in the circumstances.
And you'll have the document if I get killed. All right?

It was Scott's turn to mull things over before speaking.

Another drink before we think of dinner? he asked.

Sure, I said. Then we do have a deal?

He nodded.

When he came back with the drinks I said, I don't want you to believe that I think you're Q and I'm 007, but there are a couple of items of equipment I could use.

Speak, Captain!

I wonder whether you guys could come up with a pistol or revolver that would explode when fired. A small explosion. Enough to rip the shooter's hand off, but not so strong as to do much more damage to him or to someone standing a few feet away. The second item is a blowgun or an air pistol and darts that would paralyze someone Slobo's size, that would work if they passed through a couple of layers of clothing, and would, if possible, leave him able to speak. Being able to speak isn't important if the paralysis is of relatively short duration. But whatever agent the dart is spiked with would have to work pretty fast, in seconds.

I'm pretty sure I can provide the handgun, said Scott. It so happens that I know we have such a gadget. The tranquilizing dart is a problem. It's difficult to use. I'll have to look into how we can meet your specifications, Captain. Since you're staying in the city this weekend, I'll drop in on you and Kerry and bring whatever goodies I can find.

Before going out to dinner, Scott checked his computer. The photo came up on the screen. A full pale face with a surprisingly thin nose, on the left cheek a scar from what was likely a deep knife cut that wasn't sewn up promptly, small

blue eyes, brown hair combed back in a style that was familiar to me from travel in Greece and Turkey.

Fairly distinctive, I said, hardly a face you'd forget if you
looked at it hard.

We went to the same restaurant as on my previous visit.
Over soft-shell crabs and peas I told Scott about Bozo-on-
the-Beach, and said the guy's size and heft made me think
he was Slobo. That nose, the scar, I continued, no wonder he
wears a ski mask when he doesn't want to be remembered by
his public.

Interesting, interesting, Scott mused. This was before you
made your discoveries. Certainly before Brown had any wind
of your interest in him. Why do you suppose Slobo would be
already on your case? And if he was on your case, why do you
suppose he let it drop once you were whisked away by those
Bonackers?

I'll ask him next time we meet, I answered, and will let you
know what he tells me.

An exploding handgun. Tranquilizing darts. What
next? I asked myself. The elements of a plan were slowly and
vaguely forming in my mind but hadn't jelled into something
complete or recognizable. I knew that I was likely to have
to turn the tables on Slobo by surprising him somehow, but
when I tried to visualize the encounter with him my mind
became a blank and remained one even if I assumed, as I
had when I put on my tough-guy act for Scott, that it would
take place at Harry's house in Sag Harbor. Alternatively, my
thoughts would stray obsessively toward the scene of the

revenge killing in the Mato Grosso. Alberto Ferreira puts out the word that he'll be sitting on his porch every evening, ready to receive the thug who'd murdered his predecessor. Sure enough, one evening the guy arrives, tosses a hand grenade, and for good measure empties the magazine of his Smith & Wesson. Is Ferreira dead? Hell no: the figure in the rocker was just a dummy dressed to look like him. Meanwhile the real Alberto Ferreira lets the murderer have it with both barrels of his 12-gauge shotgun. So brilliant! Why wouldn't it work for me? Great military leaders don't try to re-invent the wheel. They study the great campaigns, whether it's Hannibal crossing the Alps or Napoleon marching on Ulm. Why couldn't I borrow a window display dummy from Ralph Lauren's men's store, where I'd spent a fortune buying a shearling coat (and inscribed to the salesman and his husband a copy of my second book), stick a wig and some clothes on the dummy, sit him down in the studio in Sag Harbor, in the very spot where Harry must have been, and lure Slobo in?

I knew the answer. The terrain and the enemy were too vastly different. To boil it down to one fact only, there was no porch in Sag Harbor on which I could rock and expose myself to Slobo's fire. Only the general concept of the trap with me as bait applied. The rest was a wild array of unknowns that I must match by flexibility and diversity of arsenal. I didn't think that Scott would be able to produce the dart I might need. If he did come up with one, it was apt to be too weak or too strong. There was another source I thought of as I was preparing to go to bed in the back bedroom of his flounder house. Susie the veterinarian! Divorced from a guy I'd played lacrosse with, she'd made a specialty of big animals and worked at the Bronx Zoo. I called her in the morning and asked if I could see her on my way from the airport. Even a modest literary celebrity, if combined with Hollywood success, is a great help when it comes to wasting the time of busy people. She gave me the directions to the Wildlife Health Center on the zoo grounds and said she'd be at her office.

Yeah, it's warm here, she said, we keep it that way for our smaller clients. The big guys, my special pets, we don't usually see here. We make house calls, she laughed. Go ahead, take off your jacket. I'll take mine off too.

I'd always thought she was pretty, but I'd never seen her look as well. Under the white coat she'd removed she had a gray sleeveless top, and I noticed that she didn't shave her armpits. Was this a new development, I wondered, or had I never had occasion to look? There was a smell of fresh sweat in the air, without a doubt her sweat. I found I was powerfully aroused, and forced myself to remember the purpose of my visit and, of course, Kerry. Meanwhile she chatted away, telling me she'd never been happier at work, that she and my former teammate Hugh were on good terms, they had an occasional drink together and made out for old times' sake but except for one time nothing below the waist, how she met guys here and there, mostly in the neighborhood bars in the East Village where she lived, and that she was planning a trip to Patagonia with a couple of colleagues.

If you do that, I told her, let me know. I spent a little over a month there last winter. Just think of me as your private trip adviser. Which brings me circuitously to the reason for my visit. Have you had experience with a big animal—I don't mean an elephant or a hippo, but for instance a big ape, an orangutan—who's gotten overexcited, however that happens, and is putting some person, let's say a member of the zoo staff, in danger? I have the impression, God knows from where, perhaps from the *Times,* that at such moments an imperturbable person in a white coat, such as you, rushes in and tranquilizes the assailant. Is that true? How does it work?

She laughed again, and asked whether I had taken to writing mystery stories.

Not exactly, I told her, but it's a parallel interest.

The dart, she said, is basically a flying syringe. The point— if you like, the needle—penetrates the skin and a little metal ball in the back of the syringe, driven by inertia, pushes the liquid into the animal. All sorts of tranquilizers and muscle relaxants are used. Curare, the agent that Amazon tribes were always putting on the tips of their arrows that they shot through blow guns, is the most famous and the best. If there isn't an overdose, the subject is temporarily paralyzed. Can't move, but retains sensation. The trick is not to administer too much unless a respirator is on hand because if the paralysis is too profound it affects the lungs and the subject will be asphyxiated. So yes, the little man or the little lady can rush in with a dart gun and stop the big cat or the orangutan or the wildebeest from doing its thing. The trick is to not administer too little or too much, and that is of course directly related to size, weight, and so on.

Music to my ears, I said. How fast do these things act?

Depends on the agent and the dosage. You can speed up

the action by poisoning the needle part of the dart itself. That gets the drug into the bloodstream faster. But once the dart is in and injects the fluid the entry into the bloodstream is pretty quick anyway.

She saw the expression on my face and added, You're loving this stuff, aren't you?

I am, I am, I answered, but there is one thing I don't understand. Why don't the police use darts in most cases instead of live rounds?

Mostly stupidity, she said, at least in my opinion. The line they spout is that a standardized dose could kill a smaller-than-average person, and that the time it takes for the dart to be effective—it's a matter of seconds—is too long. Someone will have to explain to me why the risk of an overdose is less acceptable than five rounds fired from a Glock, and how massive a volley you've got to fire to stop in his tracks a determined criminal coming at you with a firearm or a machete. If you want to know my bottom line, cops don't see themselves swaggering around with a dart gun. They want the real McCoy.

Susie, I said, will you make up for me, or buy for me if they're available ready-made, two or three darts, preferably laced with curare, that will temporarily—by that I mean anything between five minutes and half an hour—paralyze a man of my build but heavier, weighing a little over one hundred ninety pounds? The stuff needs to act fast, in fact almost instantaneously. Will you do that for me?

Holy shit, Jack, she exclaimed, what are you up to? What is this for?

All right, I said, I'll tell you the unvarnished truth. There's a guy, a professional killer, with those specifications, who's going to try to kill me. Probably in ten days. I don't want to get police protection, and I'm not sure I have enough to go on to obtain it, but believe me I haven't lost my mind and I know what I'm talking about. Of course, I could shoot the bastard, or use my knife on him, but for a whole lot of reasons, none of which is humanitarian, I may not want to. So please do this for me. I'll owe you big.

Big enough to take me away from all this for a romantic weekend in Paris?

Before I could answer, she slithered into my lap. Her body burned through mine. And I had guessed right. That smell was of her sweat. She kissed me, thrusting deep with her tongue.

Wow, I said, when I had disengaged from her mouth, this is a subject we must revisit if I survive this guy's visit. So the darts had better be good.

They will, she replied. But don't fuck up. I'm not sure what I mean by it, but don't fuck up, don't let anyone know for instance I gave you those darts. It might cost me my license and perhaps time in the big house.

I won't, I told her. When can I have them?

The day after tomorrow, she said. Give me your address. I'll drop them off, together with a dart pistol. And you don't need to be there to receive the package. I'll wait for our getaway.

Some nut called this morning, Captain Jack, Jeanette told me when I got home. A foreigner. He asked to speak to you and when I said you were out of town he went like, Oh yeah, tell him he's dead meat. I was about to yell at him but he hung up.

He is a nut, Jeanette dear, I said, and an unpleasant one. I intend to take care of him in short order. In the meantime, here is what I think you should do. You'll recognize his voice, won't you?

Yes.

Well then if he calls again just hang up. Doesn't matter how often he calls. If he leaves a message, don't erase it. Second: don't let any repairmen or similar types into the apartment unless I'm here and you've checked with me first. If there's an exception to that rule, I'll tell you. Third: deliveries of food, cleaners, and so on, only let into the kitchen deliverymen you know. If it's somebody new and I'm not at home, tell the elevator man you want the delivery held downstairs until I come back. If I'm at home, call me and let me take a look at the deliveryman.

Yes sir, Captain Jack, she said mournfully. Are you scared of this nut?

No, I'm not, I replied, but I don't want either you or me to get in trouble because we don't take precautions.

I resolved to get Kerry to adopt a similar set of rules for her apartment and to follow those that Martin had prescribed, and wolfed down the lunch Jeanette had prepared. I'd read the *Times* on the plane so I took a second cup of coffee with me to my study and called Simon Lathrop. It had occurred to me that Brown must be content to have his legal flank secure, with Will Hobson in control of J & W. It was time to rattle his cage and initiate some activity at the firm.

Abner Brown is a real bastard, I told Simon. It's astonishing that Harry was able to get along with him—no, put up with him—for so many years.

No doubt you saw the foulmouthed rough version, Simon replied. I know it exists. In fact Harry described it. But there is another side that's all quirky charm and considerateness and, don't forget it because it's all important if you want to understand Harry, a truly remarkable talent for business and very high intelligence. A highly sophisticated collector, with genuine personal taste! And not just his admirable Renaissance bronzes. Early Florentine painting as well, a major collection. That's one side of the equation. On the other were Harry's love for handling the most challenging business problems, of which Brown had plenty, his ambition, which made him want to get the Brown business and hang on to it, and his loneliness. Until you came back from Afghanistan, for many years, Brown really furnished Harry's life.

And after all that, Brown turned on him, I interjected. Turned on him viciously.

Simon laughed and said, That is definitely not out of character. On the contrary!

All things considered, I continued, my conversation with him went pretty much as expected. You'll be interested to hear that he flatly denies having asked that Harry stop working on his matters because he thought Harry had lost his marbles. Instead, he gave me to understand he fired Harry because Harry had confronted him about illegalities Harry had discovered. That is very different from the story that Will Hobson gave me.

Indeed, Simon said, after a silence, very different. What

you're saying squares with other anomalies in Hobson's activities. None of this could have happened when we still functioned like a real partnership and partners—especially the seniors—really kept an eye on what was going on inside the firm. Now the chairman and his handpicked management committee can play it pretty close to the vest. But I'm ready to convene another meeting of the senior group in the firm for the purpose of starting a formal inquiry. It would not be unusual to ask an eminent outsider, a former federal judge or U.S. attorney, to head it up. You're no longer asking that I delay?

Not at all, I replied. So far as I'm concerned, the sooner the better.

I told Kerry almost everything about the visit to Brown Tower and what I'd learned about Slobo from Scott, leaving out my speculations about Slobo's likely course of action. She grew very serious and, for the second time since I've known her, began to cry. I'm so scared, I'm so scared, I don't want them to kill you, was what she repeated over and over. Why can't you be reasonable? Let's take what you have—Harry's notes that you've put in that safe-deposit box included—and go to see the U.S. attorney. If you let me look at the notes I'll confirm that it's the dynamite we think it is, but even without a look, knowing Harry, I'm sure it's very serious stuff. Let them start an investigation into Harry's death, into Brown, and let them give you serious police protection. You owe me this, Jack. You've told me you love me, you've said you want to marry me, and I want to marry you too, you have no right to act like some crazy Wild West sheriff who's got to get his man. You've been to Iraq, you've been to Afghanistan, it's enough!

The only answer I could come up with was that she had to trust me. Slobo wouldn't kill me, I'd kill him. And then we'd live happily ever after.

And what if Slobo doesn't come after you alone, she wailed, what if this isn't some sort of shootout where you can show you're the fastest gun in the West, what if you go to Sag Harbor and they toss hand grenades in through the window or do any of the other things where it won't matter how strong, how brave, how clever you are? Do you think Harry would want you to die that way?

I've gone beyond the point of no return, I answered. Having told Brown to send me Slobo so I could kill him, I can't back out.

You'll be dead, and he'll just laugh, laugh, and laugh.

There was nothing to be done.

I told her that Scott was coming to town that weekend and we agreed to take him to the ballet and dinner afterward on Saturday. The following weekend, though, Western Industries, her big client, was holding a management retreat in Edgartown, on Martha's Vineyard. Having been asked to give a presentation on corporate legal compliance, she was obliged to go. I congratulated her, and said I'd take advantage of her being busy to scoot over to Sag Harbor and arrange for some planting in the garden. We slept together that night joylessly, holding on to each other for dear life, and that was the pattern until she left for Martha's Vineyard. I drove her once again to the Marine Terminal where she caught the shuttle for Boston's Logan Airport. Western Industries' jet was taking her and the top management from there to the Vineyard. On the way to the terminal, I told her I'd be there to pick her up when she returned on Sunday evening. I don't think she was fooled by this attempt to reassure her.

Right after Kerry left for the office, I checked messages on my landline. I found there was one. I thought it might be Slobo. But no, it was my agent, asking if I'd be willing to appear on Lou Brennan's Sunday morning show on Fox News. He's gotten a sneak look at your new book and would really like to talk to you about it. I think I know the answer, but still . . .

She thought, quite reasonably, that wild horses couldn't drag me to a Fox News show—and indeed they wouldn't have, under normal circumstances. But this, I realized, could be a godsend.

Do you mean this coming Sunday?

Yes, his producer knows it's short notice, but they'd really like it.

All right, I said, tell him I'll be there!

I didn't think Kerry or Scott would mind if I disappeared for part of the morning.

Television hosts interviewing an author have rarely read his books. This interview was different. Brennan seemed to have read my book and liked it, and was so eager to talk about it that I thought we'd never get to the one subject that

I wanted to talk about. Finally we did: my plans for the weeks and months to come, which I narrowed down to my plans for the following weekend. I laid them out laboriously, brooking no interruption. Filibusters succeed on talk shows almost as well as in the U.S. Senate.

I'm going to my house in Sag Harbor, I announced, quite alone, to do some planting in the garden but mostly to attend to unfinished family business. The house belonged to my beloved uncle, Harry Dana, who died last January in circumstances that have not been elucidated to my satisfaction. I am working hard to make them generally known and understood. That won't interfere with my routine.

You have a routine you follow? Brennan interjected.

Absolutely. It may be the result of my Marine Corps training and experience. I'll get to my house around ten on Friday night, make myself some scrambled eggs, wash them down with bourbon, and go to sleep. Of late, I've made it a habit to sleep in what was my uncle's studio, in the garden, which is, incidentally, where he died. The next morning, I'll run on the beach. Gibson Lane, in Sagaponack. Then I'll putter around in the garden, do some writing, take a nap in that studio, and go out to dinner. And after dinner to bed! Sunday morning, same deal, unless it's raining, in which case I'll be in my studio writing. I'm a maniac for routine, and I've adopted some of my uncle's habits. Some are downright silly. Like not ever locking the front door when I'm in Sag Harbor. There's nothing in that house to steal, unless you count a twelve-year-old TV set. And if anybody wants to mess with me, they're welcome!

. . .

Brennan seemed content and so was the producer, and I was delighted. If there was one TV channel Brown and his minions watched it was surely Fox News. I'd announced my schedule loud and clear. All they had to do was to make sure Slobo knew it. I was ready for him. As he'd promised, Scott brought the booby-trapped revolver. It's a beauty, he said. I saw its brother tested. It's just the kind of explosion you want. The guy loses a hand and little else—oh, maybe an eye if he's unlucky. He didn't bring the darts. The lab claims the results aren't uniform enough for them to recommend the use of curare. I thanked him, and said not to worry. Susie had dropped off her darts and something told me that what was sauce for an orangutan was also sauce for Slobo.

XIII

'd told my housekeeper Mary that I'd be arriving in Sag Harbor Friday evening, after the IGA had closed, and asked her to buy and put in the fridge a dozen eggs, a stick of butter, a baguette, and three low-fat Swiss yogurts. She'd done that and had put lilacs, the first of the season in the Hamptons, I supposed, in vases on the kitchen table, in my bedroom, and in the study. A quick tour of the house showed that, as usual, it was spick-and-span. That young woman was a gem. Just enough light remained for a quick look at the garden. The forsythia bushes were in full bloom; the lilacs were beginning to stir. On the surface, all was very well, but the house felt unloved and unloving, as though Harry's unappeased ghost were abroad, and the house itself knew that a curse had been laid upon it. I renewed my resolve to lift it during the two days that followed. The car was parked in the street, where I'd left it. I put it in the garage. I didn't particularly want to be surprised by Slobo after I went to bed and it occurred to me that even though I wasn't locking the front door I might set the alarm, disabling the motion in the house feature. But I decided against it. If Slobo tripped the alarm when he opened the front door, the siren might scare him off. We didn't want that. Nor, if he persisted, did we want the police barging in on us. I decided against the alarm. My light sleep had stood me in good stead at least twice, when the Taliban got inside our perimeter in Helmand, and then my fatigue had been far greater.

The store-window dummy, whom I'd taken to calling Morris, was in the back of the Audi. Eagerness to try him out got the better of my hunger. I brought him in, dressed him in one of my blue canvas L.L. Bean shirts, and put the wig on his head. Stretched out on his side on the sofa in the studio, facing the wall, curled up under the lightweight comforter, he was a dead ringer for me. I didn't like the expression in this particular context, but couldn't resist it. Besides it gave me a good laugh. This unprogrammed activity completed, I returned to the schedule with which I'd acquainted Fox News viewers. I hadn't had a bite since the tuna salad I'd eaten at the Irish pub on Third Avenue two blocks down from the gym, and I was seriously starved. My trainer, Wolf, and I had gone through a spirited hour-and-a-half session of Krav Maga, the Israeli Defense Forces form of martial arts. Try to kill me, I told him. Do it or you're roadkill. He didn't like that concept and went at me with all he had. We fought to a draw. The workout had been so good, I told him, that if I scraped through an appointment I had that weekend I'd treat him to the best steak dinner money could buy in New York.

There was no one in my kitchen to say *tsk-tsk*. Feeling

not the least bit guilty, I scrambled six eggs and wolfed them down with four pieces of buttered toast. There was more than enough bourbon in the liquor cabinet. It would have made my TV host Brennan proud to see me go at it. I'd brought the *Times* from the city and zipped through the first section as I drank my coffee. Only one cheerful piece of news stood out: Boris Johnson had been reelected to a second term as mayor of London. So far as I was concerned, he and Mike Bloomberg could be mayors for life. As for the rest, it confirmed the abysmal idiocy of Western involvements in the Middle East and Afghanistan, reflexive actions leading to humiliation and disaster. I decided against a fourth bourbon and laid out my equipment. The dart pistol, the darts, and the antidote went into a tote suspended from a coat hook in the front hall. Scott's revolver had arrived in a plastic box. I didn't know whether all fingerprints had been wiped off it, but I certainly didn't want mine on it. For that matter, I had no idea whether it was registered and, if it was, in whose name. Perhaps it made no difference. Anyway, I wasn't about to call Scott to inquire. I opened the box, pulled on kitchen rubber gloves, and put the revolver on a side table next to the sofa on which my friend Morris was reposing. Easy for him to grab it if his slumber was interrupted, I figured. My switchblade was in my pocket. The .45 and my Ka-Bar were in my duffel bag along with night-vision goggles. The line about choosing to give up my bedroom and sleep in the studio was bullshit: disinformation for the consumption of whoever had watched Brennan's program and especially Slobo and his handlers.

. . .

I slept hard, and might have slept through any visit Slobo chose to make, and certainly past eight, if Mary hadn't called to ask whether everything at the house was as I wished. Had I changed my mind and would let her work at the house today? I said she was a love but I could manage just fine provided she didn't mind if the house was a mess when I left for the city on Sunday. Reluctantly I got up, made a pot of strong coffee, drank most of it, went back upstairs, got into my running togs, and put the switchblade in the pocket of my windbreaker. I was almost out the front door when I realized I shouldn't leave Morris on the sofa, or, for that matter, the revolver on the table. What if Slobo came to reconnoiter while I was out? Cursing, I took apart the installation in the studio and stowed the dummy in a downstairs coat closet that I didn't think would be of interest to my Serb guest. That done, I got the car out of the garage, pulled down the garage door as Harry always did because he thought leaving it open looked untidy, and drove to the ocean.

It was a perfect beach day: sunny, windless, and fresh, with the car's thermometer showing sixty-two, and I was surprised not to see any cars at the Gibson Lane entrance. I locked the Audi, did some stretches, and ran east. The bourbon I'd consumed had left no trace, no lingering headache, no suspicious taste in my mouth. Since I had plenty of time, I decided I'd go as far as the East Hampton main beach. Round-trip, that made almost twelve miles. I intended to call Sasha and ask to have dinner with her, but I didn't think I should disturb her before ten-thirty. Trying hard to be polite as I ran, I nevertheless scattered congregation after congregation of seagulls. Soon, I thought, it would be time for plovers, the elegant tiny birds that nest in the dunes and sprint along the water's edge, haughtily indifferent to intruders like me. Perhaps they'll be there already next weekend, I thought, when Kerry will come here with me. We'll run Saturday and Sunday, first thing in the morning. These thoughts of happiness to come were interrupted by an aura that told me of a presence close by of someone I had neither seen nor heard. Without slowing down, I turned and saw him, perhaps a hundred paces behind me. It was he. No question about it. Same silver-gray running suit, same ski mask. Bozo-on-the-Beach redivivus! Or rather, as I was now certain, Slobo. This was not the encounter I had imagined or prepared for, but a great sense of relief came over me, bordering on exultation. Why not conclude it here and now, on this glorious strand that had been Harry's? I grasped the switchblade and, palming it unopened, turned and dropped into a crouch. With my other hand, I scooped up just enough sand to throw into Slobo's eyes when he closed in.

Come on, you son of a bitch, I yelled, let's do it!

He stopped too, yelled back something I couldn't understand, and reached into the pocket of his hoodie. I wondered whether it would be a knife or a gun. If it was a gun, he and his employer were right, I was dead meat; if a knife I thought it more likely that I'd eat him for my second breakfast. It was neither: he brought out a stick of chewing gum, peeled it, stuck it in his mouth, put the crumpled wrapper back in his pocket, and gave me the finger. The fuckhead liked that gesture. Then, with a lightness of step and speed that were astonishing for someone of his size and heft, he sprinted up the dune and out of sight. I didn't follow. Either it was a stupid-ass ambush, one that would have allowed him to jump me from the back, or an invitation to a wild-goose chase. There is a road that services the houses sitting behind the dune. Doubtless he had a car parked on it. In this early season, many of these summer residences were likely to be empty even on Saturday. He would have found one with no sign of life in it, used the terrace or a gazebo as a stake-out, and rushed from there to the beach when he saw me. Since I'd given no sign of walking into whatever trap he had intended, in all likelihood he was already in his car, savoring the prospect of the visit that I was now sure he'd pay me later in the day or at night. What was the point of harassing me on this beach this morning or weeks ago when I first saw him? I'd no idea. Perhaps he thought he'd psych me out.

No longer carefree, I completed my run, drove home, and called Sasha. She was free, brushed aside my offers to take her out to the American Hotel or the Thai restaurant, and invited me instead to dinner at her house.

Seven, she said. I know it's early for you, but I'm a country mouse.

I told her she had a deal.

In fact, it suited me to have dinner at Sasha's house: since I wouldn't be using my car, and planned to get to her place through the garden gate, Slobo—probably staked out this time in a parked car—would not be able to tell for sure whether or when I had left my own house, where I had gone, or when I had returned. The days were already long. I could be easily having dinner in the kitchen without electric lights, so that the house being dark would not necessarily indicate that I wasn't there. The studio was another issue. If I was at home, I would have almost certainly turned on a reading lamp there. But that was a light Slobo wouldn't be able to see from the street, or through Harry's fence and hedge enclosing the garden if he tried to snoop in the back alley. As for Sasha's dinner being early, that was fine too. I was impatient for the bastard to strike. If nothing happened during the afternoon, for instance during my supposed nap, he'd attack at night. We'd meet after I came home. The early dinner would shave an hour or two from the wait for the moment that would decide my fate and his. I showered and dressed, got at the IGA oranges and grapes for tomorrow's breakfast, carried them home, and went out again, this time for a sandwich. When I returned, I checked carefully for signs of an interim visit. It was as I had expected. Nothing had been disturbed. I transferred the .45, the dart pistol and its accessories, and the Ka-Bar knife to the studio, and put them on the desk. I had borrowed from Kerry a voice recorder she sometimes used to dictate time sheets at her apartment. Not knowing whether it was fully charged, I plugged it into the surge-protector strip under the desk, connected my laptop alongside it, and got to work. I was writing the first of the four portraits of men in my platoon in Fallujah who didn't make it. They were to be my new book. I worked steadily until six.

Kerry had told me that the Western Industries program in Edgartown called for a Saturday cocktail hour on the porch of the Harbor View Hotel. It seemed to me that there could be no objection to a hotshot lawyer's receiving a phone call while those festivities were in progress. If I was wrong, she wouldn't answer and I'd leave a message. But she answered almost immediately, sounding anxious and relieved.

Wait one second, she whispered over the roar of the party. I'm moving to where there's less noise.

When she spoke again, it was to ask: Are you all right? I'm worried sick.

I told her that I was fine and unworried, that I was going to dinner at Sasha's, and that I was making plans for our runs on Gibson Lane Beach, as well as for indoor activities that might turn out to be even more pleasurable. Next weekend, I specified. Please don't develop any impossible-to-break business engagements. Not even for the greater glory of Western Industries or Jones & Whetstone.

You make a joke of everything, she scolded gently, but this isn't a laughing matter. Have you seen him?

In a manner of speaking, yes, but nothing happened, I answered, and I want you to stop fretting about it. All will be well. I'll see you at the airport tomorrow. And don't forget we have a date tomorrow night and every night next week.

She had a hundred recommendations for how I should be careful and should call her before going to sleep, no matter how late it was. I promised to do both.

I decided to leave the dart pistol, the darts, and the anti-dote in the half-open drawer of the desk in the studio, but moved the .45 and the Ka-Bar back to the tote in the front hall. Then I grabbed a can of WD-40 oil in the garage, and carefully sprayed the front door hinges. When I tried it, the door opened and shut with no more noise than a knife going through butter. After going back and forth about it in my mind, I reinstalled Morris on the studio couch, with Scott's revolver within his reach. There was no way of foreseeing how his presence would play out. There was a slight chance that Slobo might be fooled, with consequences if I wasn't there I couldn't foresee. In the worst case, Morris would only puzzle Slobo, or perhaps put him in a rage because he'd think I was fucking with him. The truth is that I didn't care. These tasks done, I took a shower, got dressed, and went over to Sasha's through the garden gate, the switchblade in the pocket of my jacket, and an orchid plant I'd bought on my way home from lunch in my hand. I had left the front door unlocked. That was how Harry had always done it, that is what I'd said on Fox I'd do, and that is what Slobo had every right to expect.

Coming home from Sasha's, I entered the house through the front door, paused, and listened carefully. The house was still as a tomb. But there was something else. I have a very keen sense of smell, permanently sharpened, as apparently it often happens, by hepatitis I caught as a boy during a family vacation in Turkey. The odor I was detecting of unwashed underclothes, stale sweat, and tobacco could have only one source. I took off my shoes, reached for the Ka-Bar and the .45, and slipped them into my waistband. My night-vision goggles were also in the tote. I put them on and sniffed again. Mixed with the stench I'd identified was a separate smell, that of turpentine, the same odor as in Sasha's studio where we had looked at her new work and had drinks before dinner. The two came from the same direction, from the hallway and the dining room. Noiselessly—the oak floors in Harry's house did not creak—I followed. The French windows in the dining room that gave on the garden, which I had shut before leaving the house, were open. Pistol in hand, Ka-Bar in my waistband, I stepped through them and advanced slowly toward the studio.

He'd left the door open and in the moonlight that flooded the studio through the skylight I could see him distinctly. The same silhouette: without a doubt the man I had twice seen on the beach. For this occasion, he'd exchanged his silver-gray outfit for black. A black jean jacket, black jeans flaring over black engineer boots, and a black ski mask made of some shiny fabric. He must have just arrived. Legs wide apart, a round leather body blackjack perhaps a foot long in his right hand, a can of turpentine in the other, he stood before the sofa, apparently bemused by the recumbent figure.

You sleep, dead meat, he finally uttered, you sleep good? I help sleep better!

With that, he raised the blackjack and brought it down on Morris's head with measured force that I judged would not have broken my skull but would have left me out cold much longer than required for his project. I'd fooled him! It helped that my dummy friend's head was some kind of solid rubber. What Slobo was up to became plain when he unscrewed the top of the can and began to squirt the liquid on the huge Turkish kilim. Pax, Ian Fleming! The men dispatching hardened criminals aren't all deviant geniuses. This idea was so simple and so stupid. A banal accident: the bestselling author

and decorated former Marine officer John Chilton Dana
died of burns and asphyxiation in a conflagration that consumed with devastating speed the secondary residence he
maintained in Sag Harbor, New York, the scene also several
months earlier of the suicide of his uncle, Harold Chilton
Dana, a prominent New York attorney. The interesting question was how Slobo intended to start the fire. I didn't think
it would be a lighted match or his Zippo lighter, although I
was sure that as a heavy smoker he owned one. More likely,
he had thought of an electric short. The whack he'd given my
double on the sofa gave him plenty of leisure to work on that
one. Killers for hire often have another profession. Perhaps
in some early avatar, before hooking up with Karadžić, he'd
been an electrician. But really, it was so too bad! Hard luck on
Slobo! I wasn't going to give him a chance to show his stuff
by completing that phase of his assignment. My assignment,
as I now saw it, was to give him an opening to attack, and to
make him think he'd nailed me. I stuck the .45 in my waistband out of sight and snug against my spine and drew the
Ka-Bar.

All right, Slobo, I called out. Stop messing with my rug.
And drop the blackjack.

He wheeled around, dropping the can but not the club.
With his free hand he snatched the ski mask off his head
and threw it on the ground as well. It was the face I had seen
on Scott's computer, now contorted in a snarl that bared his
teeth.

Fuck you, dead meat! he spat out. You try get me! You
think you make fool of Slobo! I beat shit out of you. I make
you crawl in your shit till you beg to be dead.

You wanted to butcher my uncle? I returned. I think I'll start by cutting you.

He advanced on me with the speed I had already observed and aimed a blow at the side of my head. The Krav Maga session with Wolf had not been a waste of time. I ducked under his arm, and lunging from the side cut him on his right arm, the arm that wielded the blackjack.

You like that? I asked. You want more? You're a dead duck, Slobo Milić. The feds know who you are. For you there's no way out. You've got a one-way ticket to the electric chair. Now drop the fucking blackjack.

His answer was to charge me. I pivoted and escaped the full impact, but the pain of the glancing blow to my shoulder blade was extreme, making me wonder whether he'd hit Harry with that thing. In such a case, I couldn't blame Harry for not wanting to take more blows. I retreated toward the desk. The arm I had cut was bleeding heavily enough for drops of blood to drip down the sleeve of Slobo's denim jacket, but he rushed me again, aiming a wild haymaker once more at the side of my skull. This time I ducked successfully and cut him again, thrusting the Ka-Bar into his forearm.

He stopped, transferred the blackjack into his left hand, and with his right drew a knife from under the jacket. Come here dead meat! he called. Now you finished.

I have a better idea, I answered, grabbing the dart pistol. Listen carefully, Slobo! I want you to drop the blackjack and drop the knife. Then I need you to sit down on the sofa and talk to me. If you do that, I'll give you a tourniquet for your arm. If you don't, I'll shoot you with a dart. It's loaded with curare and will paralyze you. You won't be able to move, but you will feel everything. In particular, you will feel it when I cut your ears, nose, and balls off and do a lot of the other fun stuff you and your friends did in Srebrenica.

His answer, which I had been praying for, was to retreat slowly and carefully, to lurch to the left, and with the suddenness of an uncoiling spring seize Scott's pistol.

You dumb fuck, he said, transferring the pistol to his right hand. You leave gun where I can get? You drop that fucking toy, drop the knife, and get down on knees. Hands behind head.

This was the moment to take the risk. As I charged him wordlessly, I heard the explosion and felt the impact of a hit just above my right eyebrow. That I should be grateful I didn't lose an eye was something I knew at some deep level, but my vision and attention were riveted to Slobo. He was howling, holding his right arm reduced by the explosion to a stump from which gushed a stream of blood.

Tough luck, Slobo! I cried. Now do as I say. Drop the knife, take off your jacket, and sit down. I'll give you a tourniquet, and if you behave I'll call 911 and get you help.

He stared at me dumbly, slowly dropped the knife, and began to unbutton his jacket. Realizing in a flash what might be coming I reached for my .45, withdrew it from my waistband, and held it out of Slobo's sight. My instinct had been right. From under his jacket, held in his left hand, appeared a Browning pistol.

Now I kill you, dead meat! he yelled.

At the same time, I fired. My aim was good. I shot the Browning out of his hand. With it went one or more of his fingers.

Keeping him covered, I backed into the bathroom, grabbed a hand towel, and returning to the main room cut it into two strips.

Do you want to put a tourniquet on that arm, I asked, or would you rather just bleed?

Tourniquet, he answered through clenched teeth, tourniquet.

I threw him the strip and told him how to wrap it just below the elbow and with his left hand, wounded but still usable, twist it until the worst of the bleeding stopped. He followed my instructions with great energy, I would almost say goodwill. When he had finished I told him to hold out the left hand. I bandaged it quickly. That done, I ordered him to sit down in one of the armchairs.

The telephone rang at this point. It was Sasha. She'd heard twice, coming from the direction of my house, a noise that could be a firecracker—but this wasn't a season for firecrackers—or a firearm. Was I all right? Should she call the police? I assured her that everything was under control. We'd talk in the morning.

Oh good, she answered, forgive me for being a worrywart. You know I'll never forgive myself for not doing something that night when Harry died.

After I'd hung up, .45 in my right hand because I didn't trust Slobo's new docility, I turned on the voice recorder and said, Now you're going to talk. I'll record you. You don't know it, but my uncle recorded you. That's how I found out what you did to him.

You get ambulance, he stammered.

I will, I said, I will. But not before you've answered my questions. So be quick about it. Your name?

Slobodan Milić.

Did you kill Harry Dana in this house in January by forcing him to hang himself?

The shithead? I kill him. He give me no trouble.

And you tortured and killed his cat. Right?

Fucking queer. Yeah I kill cat. I fuck cat too, but asshole too small.

And Barbara Diamond. Did you push her under the subway train the next day?

The fat pig? I push her.

Who sent you to do it? Mr. Abner Brown?

I don't know any fucking Abner Brown.

So who do you work for?

Boss in my country. In Serbia.

Who is he? What's his name?

I don't tell. I tell you, they kill me. You kill me, they kill me, no difference. I don't betray. You call ambulance now?

And they're the same people who sent you to kill me?

Same people, he answered. The shithead hangs himself. The fat pig falls under a train. You die in fire. You call the ambulance now?

Any minute now, I said. First tell me this: did you hear anything about who hired your people in Serbia?

A rich guy. A rich guy in Texas. I don't know name.

And why did you come after me on the beach? Weeks ago, before you were hired to kill me?

Because I hear the shithead is your uncle and you're fucking marine officer. Fucking marines kill my kid brother in Bosnia. I hate marine guts. Like I call you in your fucking apartment.

So why didn't you kill me on the beach? First time or second time, you schmuck?

First time I have no order to kill. Second time I have order. You die in accident. You get ambulance now?

I switched off the voice recorder and said, Not yet, not now. You haven't told me the whole truth about Abner Brown, and you haven't told me for whom you work in Serbia. You haven't kept your part of the bargain. But I'm willing to give you a drink or two.

He wanted whiskey, no ice. I gave him a double shot and then another.

I turned on the classical music station on the radio, and we sat there peacefully. He asked for another drink. I gave it to him and poured one for myself.

I take off tourniquet, he said at some point. Arm change color.

Good idea, I replied. Just make yourself comfortable.

Meanwhile, I watched him carefully. When his face had lost all color and he began to slump, I called 911 and reported an armed attack on me at my house, which I had been able to repel. The assailant had lost considerable blood. The police dispatcher took down the information and said she'd be sending a cruiser and an ambulance.

One of the paramedics asked whether I realized my face was covered with blood. I said truthfully that I hadn't. He washed off the wound and put a dressing on it, after which the paramedics left, removing Slobo on a stretcher. He was alive but unconscious. Meanwhile, the police poked around the studio in a desultory fashion. Having taken my statement, and verified that the .45 was registered to me, the police sergeant in charge observed that I was lucky to be alive, and asked that I leave the crime scene undisturbed in case the D.A. wanted to examine it. I assured him I would. As soon as the police left, I called Kerry. It was past midnight, and I could tell that she was wide-awake.

It's all right, I told her. Everything is just fine. I'll see you tomorrow. Can't wait!

Jack, she said, you're holding everything back. What happened? Did Slobo appear?

Yes, I answered, he made his swan song after what I'm sure has been a long and rich career. All kidding aside, he did pay me a visit. The paramedics and the police have been here as well. Slobo has left in an ambulance, and now they're gone too. I guess they're driving him to the hospital in Southampton, it being the nearest, but it really doesn't matter. He won't make it to there any more than to Riverhead or Stony Brook.

After we'd said good night, and I'd told her for the tenth time that I loved her, I realized that I had been crowing. I had not managed to filter out of my voice my immense and shameless self-satisfaction.

Unless her sleep was preternaturally profound, Sasha had of course seen and heard the police and the ambulance arrive at my house in the night. I called her first thing next morning—earlier than I would have normally dared to—reassured her that I was perfectly all right, and asked if

I might come over to have a cup of coffee and explain the strange goings-on. She sat at her kitchen table still as a statue as I told her the real story of Harry's death, the torture of Plato, and Slobo's visit the night before. After I'd finished, speaking in a tiny, strangled voice she offered me another cup of coffee and, as though the effort to speak had proved too much for her strength, began to cry. She cried noisily, without any effort to control herself, a lamentation the likes of which I had witnessed in Greece, one of which I would not have thought a proper Bostonian of her generation would have been capable. I didn't try to tell her to stop. Instead, I pulled my chair to her side and put my arm around her shoulders and held her until slowly both her trembling and her tears stopped.

She asked to be excused while she washed her face. When she returned I said, Sasha there is something I think we should do. I have Harry's ashes in the house. Would you like to come with me later this morning and scatter them in the surf of Gibson Beach? I think Harry would have liked that. And there is another thing. Mary has Plato's ashes. I'd like to call her and ask her to bring his ashes and join us. Cats don't exactly like the ocean, but in this case . . . I think both Plato and Harry would approve.

Yes, she said, they would both like that. Let's do it. And afterward let's all three have a stiff gin martini. Just the way Harry made them. And I'll propose a toast to you, in honor of what you've done.

XIV

took advantage of the interval between Slobo's passing out and the arrival of the police to do some housekeeping. Morris went into the coat closet. I could see no useful purpose being served by a meeting between him and the forces of order. The dart pistol, the darts, and the antidote went into the cupboard in the dining room. On the deepest level, I was convinced that I had nothing to hide. Slobo had come to kill me. Acting in self-defense, I'd wounded him. If he died, that was his bad luck. Had I wrongfully withheld first aid? No I hadn't. I'd given him a tourniquet for one arm and had bandaged the other. Had I acted illegally by not calling 911 sooner? I didn't know whether there was a duty to rush to the telephone to get help for a hit man who'd just tried to murder you, but if there was such an obligation my failure to meet it was surely minor. My conversation with Slobo—interrogation, if someone wanted to be malicious—took minutes. If he died on the way to the hospital or in intensive care it would be because of the wound he'd suffered, the equivalent of an amputation. I'd seen men die on the battlefield of just such wounds. All too often, medics were unable to stop the bleeding or to provide an adequate transfusion. And was I guilty of some noxious-sounding crime, manslaughter or attempted manslaughter, because I'd put within Slobo's reach the CIA's marvelous trick handgun? I thought I could only congratulate myself on having asked Scott for it, and on having a friend able to provide such a piece of equipment. I'd spent enough time with Harry to have heard ad nauseam the old saw: the Law is an ass. I was willing to grant its truth, but even New York State law could not be asinine enough to imply a warranty of safety for a guy who comes to kill you. A promise that the gun he fires at you won't blow up in his face!

That these reflections were not off base was proved by the events of the days that followed. Slobo died in the ambulance before reaching Southampton. The police sergeant stopped by the next morning just as I was setting off for my run to say he had no further questions for me. Moses Cohen proved he was worth his salt as an all-around lawyer, able to deal with the problems of the living as well as with those of the dead. I called him Monday morning, right after Kerry left for her office, related the events of Saturday night, and asked what if anything I should do about the Suffolk County district attorney. He swung into action. It turned out that there was a lawyer in Riverhead who knew every plugged-in lawyer in the county. Moses sought his assistance regularly in connection with the zoning problems of his hedge-fund clients. Sure enough, the zoning lawyer had a partner who specialized in criminal law—principally keeping those same hedge-fund managers, their wives, and their kiddies out of jail when caught driving while under the influence, and preventing the revocation of their driver's licenses. He ran over to the D.A.'s office and returned in no time with the good news that the case was closed. In fact, it had never been opened.

So that was that. Later that morning, without telling Kerry or Scott that such was my plan lest they try to stop me, I called Abner Brown from my apartment, on my own land-line. Marvels never cease. The honey-voiced assistant put me right through to him.

Hello there, Brown, I said, I'm calling to offer my condolences. And I may be bringing news. I'm in fine shape. But your pal Slobo is good and dead. I'm sure you'll miss him. For my part I can't say I will. Have you got someone else lined up to try to kill me?

The moment of silence on the other end of the line made me think that perhaps I was indeed telling him something he didn't know.

Then he spoke more slowly than usual. Listen, you dumb fuckhead. I'm going to ask you once again. What is it you want? How do I get you to go away and stay away?

Short of having someone kill me? There is no way. But I'll tell you what I want. I want you behind bars. And that's a project on which I'm starting right now.

With that I hung up.

I made two more calls that morning. I'd spoken to Scott Sunday morning when I came back from my undisturbed beach run to tell him that I was alive and Slobo was dead, and we'd agreed to speak again on Monday to make arrangements about the contents of the safe-deposit box

I'd opened. He checked his calendar. It was a busy week but he thought he could come to New York on Wednesday afternoon and leave for D.C. the next morning on the seven o'clock shuttle.

Don't think for a moment that I'm lacking in curiosity, he added. That will be also a good time for you to fill me in on the details of Slobo's demise.

I understood the need for discretion in our telephone conversations. He was speaking from his office, and his calls were doubtless recorded. He'd given me to understand that the same was true of his official BlackBerry as well as his personal landline in Alexandria and his personal iPhone.

Next I telephoned Simon Lathrop and said I badly needed to see him.

Lunch, he asked, or would you rather come to my office?

The nature of what I want to discuss is such, I replied, that if at all possible I'd like to meet at my apartment. Can I induce you to come to lunch at Fifth Avenue? Jeanette will prepare something to make the trip uptown worthwhile.

Jeanette! he exclaimed. So you've kept her on. In that case . . . Would late lunch, say at one-thirty, be possible?

I told him that would be perfect.

Mr. Lathrop! Jeanette was overjoyed. I know just what he likes. The same thing he and Mr. Harry always enjoyed: smoked salmon, lamb chops with creamed spinach on the side, and cut-up fruit. Poor Mr. Harry! It was like a holiday for him when Mr. Lathrop came over for a meal.

I can imagine, I said. And I think we should serve wine. I'll find a good bottle.

Simon, I said, when we sat down at the table, for a variety of reasons you'll understand as I tell the story, I wasn't able until now to be entirely open with you. I hope you'll forgive me. It was unbelievable that Harry should have committed suicide, and it was unbelievable for the best reason. Harry didn't take his own life. Abner Brown sent a killer who forced him to hang himself. This last weekend, he sent the same killer to murder me, only this time the plan backfired. I killed him instead. After lunch, I'll let you see the chain of proof. There is more to this, and I'll give you a fuller account in a moment. Finally, Harry in his suicide letter, which you haven't seen but I will show you after lunch, directed me to where he had placed what seems to be a Rosetta stone or road map to Brown's and Brown companies' illegal activities. It's not here now, I've placed it in a safe-deposit box at a bank. Quite frankly, while I think I can see this document's purpose, I don't pretend to understand it. The one person who would understand it perfectly—apart from Hobson and people working for him—is obviously Kerry. She knows the road map exists but I haven't given her an opportunity to study it. Now that Brown has made his unsuccessful move to kill me I think the time has come to go public with the road map—take it to the FBI or whoever is appropriate—and I hope you'll advise me whether I'll put Kerry in a real bind or worse by letting her at last review the document and asking for her help. Of course, my purpose is to bring Brown to justice. Not only for the murder and the attempted murder—and that part may be impossible—but for everything else. For the evil Harry wanted to stop, for the evil that brought about Brown's having him murdered.

Goodness, Simon said, that's quite a lot to absorb. My initial reaction is to congratulate you on your instincts. That being said, let's eat this delectable lunch and then over coffee let me hear and see everything else needed to enlighten me.

That's what we did. In the library, I went over the story omitting only Scott's participation in furnishing the booby-trapped revolver, showed Simon Harry's letter, and played the two recordings, the one from Harry's iPhone and the one I had made of my interrogation of Slobo.

After a long silence, Simon said, I feel sick. I think next time Abner shows up at a museum board meeting I'll strangle the son of a bitch. Now let's be serious. If this road map is the result of Harry's knowledge, as Brown's and his companies' legal counsel will allege, of confidential client information he acquired as Brown's lawyer, its revelation—to the FBI as you suggested, or to the U.S. attorney—has to be considered in the light of lawyers' professional obligations.

Kerry has spoken to me about that, I interjected. She said she had to be extremely careful not to disclose privileged information to me.

Quite right, quite right, Simon continued, I'm glad she was on top of that. There is an argument available to Brown and his businesses that the stuff you think is Harry's road map is privileged and cannot be disclosed without their permission, can't be produced in court, and so forth. I'm not an expert on the Code of Conduct that applies to New York lawyers, but there are exceptions that allow a lawyer to go public, as you put it, when the client is committing a crime and the lawyer has tried unsuccessfully to stop him. I can't believe that

one or more of the exceptions doesn't apply here, or that—
assuming that what you have been telling me is generally
accurate—Brown would be able to assert privilege.

By the way, he added, that road map or something like that
is clearly what Hobson and that idiot Minot were trying to
find when they searched Harry's papers.

I nodded.

There is another aspect of the problem, Simon continued,
and it involves me just as much as Kerry. Abner Brown and
his companies are very important clients of the firm. What
you're proposing to do, probably with Kerry's assistance and
my blessing, involves the loss of their business. I don't need
to tell you that in today's economic environment, with once-
great law firms going into bankruptcy and others shedding
partners, associates, and staff, that is not a trifling matter.
The simple answer, though, is that we're not in the practice
of law in order to close our eyes to criminal activities of our
clients. That is, by the way, very different from representing someone who has been accused of a crime. I'm sure you
understand that. Criminal defendants are entitled to counsel.
To cut to the chase, I think you should show your road map
to Kerry and see what she thinks it means to an informed
reader. She's a big girl, and you're free to tell her about our
conversation. I'd like to look at it too. Of course, I've got no
objection—I'm in no position to object—to your showing it
to your friend Scott, though I would warn you against relying on the CIA when it comes to bringing Brown to justice.
There are too many crosscurrents there, too many people
pulling strings. I think you know what I mean. It's a job for

the Justice Department. Kerry will have views as to how the U.S. attorney should be approached.

I said I would proceed exactly in accordance with his advice.

There is something more I should tell you, he added. You should know that our group of seniors met with Will Hobson last Friday. He put on a weak performance, claiming that his personal observation had convinced him that Harry's cognitive faculties had declined significantly. I don't believe anyone was favorably impressed. We are meeting again on Wednesday, the day after tomorrow, without Will. When do you plan to show the map to Kerry?

I told him it was that same day, in the afternoon.

In that case, Simon said, I will request a postponement of the senior group's meeting. We might meet instead on Friday or next Monday. I'd like to be in a position to announce to the group the existence of the road map and what you are doing with it, as well as the imminent withdrawal from the firm of the Brown business. Quite an agenda! I'll ask for Hobson's head. I hope they don't instead offer him mine. As far as I can see, there is nothing innocent about Hobson's conduct. Whether Minot is an accomplice or a compliant dope remains to be seen. However this shakes out, it will be a severe test for the firm.

By the way, he said as he was leaving. The stuff about the group of seniors is still strictly between you and me. Right?

I assured him it was.

I had one more call to make, and I made it soon after Simon left for the office. It was to Susie. I got her on her cell phone. She happened to be among the orangutans. There had to be a way of wiggling out of taking her on a romantic getaway, and I thought I'd found one.

Hey, curare man, she greeted me, are you alive or is this your ghost reaching out from the great hunting grounds?

Alive, I said, alive and calling you from the ultracivilized precincts of Fifth Avenue.

So the darts worked?

The threat that I'd use them did. The bad guy won't bother me or anyone else again. I'm keeping the darts for the next deserving visitor. Here's the thing: does curare keep its potency?

I like to hear you use that word, she laughed. Yes, it does. Watch out, I may shoot you with a little dart and have my way with you if we don't fly off to Paris pretty soon. Make your plan, curare man! Cool! That even rhymes.

I have a terrific plan. I want you to come to dinner on Wednesday. Fancy dinner, fancy restaurant, and fancy company. I'm going to introduce you to my best friend. *D'accord?*

I smell a rat, she said, but *d'accord.*

Kerry had been too happy, too distracted, when I picked her up at the airport, panting with relief that I had suffered only the cut above my eye, to grill me then about exactly what had happened between Slobo and me. But there was no ducking the subject when she came to dinner on Monday. I had asked Jeanette to prepare a cold meal. I would serve it and wash up.

Kerry wore a black silk jersey dress and perilously high heels. No words were needed to tell me she wanted to make love.

She lowered her eyelids, and I led her to the bedroom.

We were happy and exhausted and may have dozed off before deciding we'd have a drink and then perhaps taste Jeanette's dinner. When we were finally at table, speaking about Slobo and Abner Brown could no longer be avoided.

We can let Martin stand down now, don't you think? she asked. What a relief! I hate to think how much he charged you.

Worth every cent, I replied, and I think we should keep him a bit longer. Brown is a vengeful man. I have a feeling that thugs like Slobo are easily replaced. Who's to say whether he wants to send Slobo Two our way? Let's see what we do with Harry's road map and the immediate fallout before making a decision.

She nodded and said, All right, and now tell me exactly what happened on Saturday night.

It was my turn to nod and reply that I'd tell her everything, but I first wanted to mention that Scott was coming to the city on Wednesday afternoon and that I hoped she was free so that we could talk about the road map together. This was as good a time as any to speak about my conversation with Simon Lathrop, without mentioning what he had told me about his group of seniors. That was a confidence that had to be respected. She listened carefully and said that asking Simon's advice, and worrying about where the road map left her, were really thoughtful. I'm glad you've done it. I think he's right about the law and about the firm. We can't go on working for Brown. Then she consulted her iPhone. She could be free on Wednesday afternoon.

In that case, I said, let's meet here.

And then once more—I was getting so good at it that it made me sick—I told her all, including what I'd withheld before, such as the toys I'd obtained, Scott's revolver and Susie's curare, and the nightcap Slobo and I enjoyed at the end. After I'd finished, I played the recording I'd made of Slobo.

I had been watching with growing despair as a sort of curtain descended between her and me. She was picking at her dessert, mechanically drinking the wine when I refilled her glass, but with each passing minute she was more distant.

Kerry, I said, sweet Kerry, this is a terrible, violent story. A tragic story that started when that bastard killed Harry. But it's over now. Finished. What I said about Brown's perhaps sending Slobo Two is a one-in-a-thousand possibility. A reason to be careful, that's all. But really all of this is behind us.

No, it isn't, Jack, she answered. It will never be behind me. Jack, I thought you killed that bastard in self-defense, to save your own life. But that's not what happened. You disabled him after he attacked you, and that was great, just what I'd expect of a marine officer, an honest-to-God hero. But then, instead of turning him over to the police, you murdered him! Jack, that's what you did! You're not dumb. You know there are laws in this country. You had the goods on him. You had his confession against his interest on tape. He was going straight to prison for the murder of Harry and attempted murder of you, but no, you let him bleed to death, you turned murderer.

All of a sudden, the refined meal I had served her, the plans I had made for our next weekend in the country, all began to seem like a monstrously bad joke. Or worse. Like coming upon the dead Iraqis whose noses and ears my marines had cut off. I didn't turn them in for court-martial. I didn't even hand out company punishment. What was the point? The noses and the ears weren't going to grow back. I wasn't about to call the Suffolk County D.A. and turn myself in.

Kerry, I said, it's done. What's done cannot be undone. That Serb bastard tortured my uncle. He tortured my uncle's lovely cat. A cat whom I had given to Harry and whom I also loved. He was wanted by Interpol and who knows—Scott will be able to tell—how many other police forces for violent and heinous crimes. I was not content to hand him over to the D.A. and have him plea-bargain his way to twelve, fifteen years in jail. In your heart, you knew that. I never made it a secret.

She said nothing when we parted in the morning, which put in doubt our sleepover dates for the rest of the week or our weekend in Sag Harbor. My heart was heavy, and I made an effort unmatched in my experience to be gentle and forbearing in our lovemaking. The shock of hearing how I killed Slobo, I told myself, had been extreme. Perhaps she had even noticed how I was crowing when I told her on the phone that I had killed him. Her antennae picked up the most distant and most feeble signals. That I was in shock as well, because of her, was also evident. I was finding myself unable to write.

I ran and worked out at the gym with Wolf. We made a date for a boys' steak dinner the following week.

As agreed, on Wednesday afternoon I got Harry's docu-

ment from the bank—I'd grown sick of calling it a road
map—and the three of us sat down at Harry's library table to
examine it. In reality, it was Kerry who read it and explained
as she went along. It was the diagram of parallel but diamet-
rically opposed universes. One was composed of the Brown
companies with which the general public was familiar. Banks
and other financial institutions, shipping lines, mining enterprises, some of which were notorious as suspected polluters
but all of which were vastly profitable and fully engaged in
fending off allegations of illegality, an agricultural empire covering much of Latin America and Romania and Ukraine. The
other, a fun-house mirror reflection of the former, marched
hand in hand, depending on the field of activity, with North
Vietnam or Iran or Hezbollah or the Taliban and its various
permutations or al-Qaeda, and in mineral activities with a
shadowy arm of the Kremlin. The secret mechanism, easy to
state but intricate enough to have withstood the scrutiny of
leading firms of auditors, Harry appeared to have discovered
almost by accident. It consisted in the existence of twin sets
of companies, the "good" companies functioning according
to the mores, however shabby, of the marketplace, and the
"bad" twins—names and logos so similar you thought they
were the same—battening on them like so many cancers.
The catalog of crimes was endless and included drug and
arms trade, nuclear proliferation, money laundering, evasion
of sanctions, child labor, pollution on a scale not imagined
before, and human trafficking. A trail of monstrously large
payoffs by the bad twins to government officials and other
dignitaries sitting on the boards and international advisory

councils of the good twins, the placement of the officials' children, wives, siblings, and cousins in plum positions with the good twins or institutions over which Abner had leverage, an open sewer of corruption.

The involvement of governments and organizations subject to every imaginable U.S. sanction, with links to international terrorist organizations, drew a long whistle from Scott. My boys will love this, he said. It will be a pleasure to get into the innards of this business.

But he and Kerry readily agreed that the ball had to be carried by the Justice Department. She knew the U.S. attorney for the Southern District; in fact had worked directly for him when they were both assistant U.S. attorneys, he very much her senior. She said she'd make an appointment for the two of us to see him at the earliest date he could give us. Scott thought it would be best if he didn't join us. He didn't want crossed wires. What he needed urgently was a copy of the diagram and a seat next morning on the first shuttle to D.C.

With mixed feelings of gloom and relief, I announced the dinner plan for the evening, managing to say that it would be a celebration of sorts and a chance for Scott to meet the gorgeous caregiver to orangutans and tigers.

Kerry said she had to go back to the office first, and then home to dress. Scott wanted to look in on his mother.

We agreed to meet at the restaurant.

Epilogue

Kerry left me. I can't stand the way you smell when you touch me, she told me. You smell of blood.

She couldn't forget the way I killed Slobo. Or forgive me. You're sick, she kept repeating. And she'd come back to her old theme: We live in a country where there are laws. The rule of law, does that ring a bell? Slobo could have been judged and punished according to the law. But that wasn't good enough for you. You had to butcher him.

The rule of law. You bet.

Perhaps a week after Scott turned over Harry's notes to his colleagues or bosses at the agency, and Kerry and I did the same to the U.S. attorney, together with such indications as we had of Abner Brown's involvement in the murder of Harry and the assault on me, I received a call from Brown himself. Someone at Langley must have tipped him off. You fuckhead, he said, I'll get you. If it isn't this week or this month, don't think it won't come. I'll hunt you down like the varmint you are. The shithead meddling nephew of a blackmailing queer. I piss on his grave and I'll piss on yours.

Tough to do from supermax, I replied. You'd better hurry.

Will Hobson and Minot left Jones, according to Simon Lathrop in disgrace but with great profit, taking the Brown business with them to a Houston law firm where they formed the nucleus of a team to defend Brown against the storm of criminal proceedings and enforcement actions unleashed by the grand jury, the DEA, the EPA, the Treasury, and the SEC. Moses Cohen sent me links to articles in *The American Lawyer* and other sheets of that ilk extolling the Brown litigations as the stimulus rescue plan for the legal profession.

Right-wing and fundamentalist flacks and their media mouthpieces on TV and radio talk shows zeroed in on Harry's sizable contributions to the winning presidential campaign in '08 and his support of Democratic candidates in the '10 congressional election. They smeared Harry as a closeted fag, a rogue lawyer out to destroy Abner Brown because of his backing rock-solid conservative causes and candidates, all the while extolling Brown as a philanthropist and patron of hospitals and museums on a scale not seen since John D. Rockefeller. Rebuffed and put in his place by Abner Brown, the narrative went, who indignantly rejected his dastardly attempts at blackmail, and faced with the loss of Brown business, Harry Dana hanged himself, following the example set by Judas.

The reputation of the dead is like a soccer ball kids kick about in an empty lot. No slander or libel laws protect it.

Meanwhile, the tabloids extolled my courage and martial skills. The typical headline trumpeted: "America's Leading Young Writer and War Hero Fights Off Dangerous Armed Assailant." Lou Brennan had me back on his Fox News show and showed deep concern that the murderer could have taken advantage of the revelations about my schedule in Sag Harbor I'd made so innocently during our previous interview. Even the *Times* devoted half a column to the troubling instance of criminal activity in the peaceful village of Sag Harbor that had put my exemplary courage to the test.

No problem. I am a warrior.

My effort at matchmaking succeeded. Susie left the Bronx Zoo to live with Scott in his flounder house in Alexandria. Her new job is at the National Zoo, and her new specialty is the loving care of pandas. Bucking the current trend, Scott and she intend to marry. He's asked me to be the best man.

My writer's block receded. I was able to finish the portraits of my four marine brothers. The book has been accepted for publication by my editor.

But it proved too difficult to write, or even pass weekends, at the house in Sag Harbor. My hope to lift the curse hanging over it has not been fulfilled.

I've taken refuge in a locanda on Torcello, where many years ago Harry used to spend a week each September. Visits to the basilica and the study of its great mosaic of the Last Judgment have been my sole distraction. It is on that tiny lagoon island that I have written much of this story and ruminated on the rule of law in my country in the second decade of the twenty-first century.

ACKNOWLEDGMENTS

The author is profoundly grateful to his friend Matthew Blumenthal, who served as an infantry officer in the United States Marine Corps; his friend and law partner Mark P. Goodman; and his friend and physician, Daniel I. Richman, for drawing on their fields of expertise to offer him comments and suggestions of inestimable value.

A NOTE ABOUT THE AUTHOR

Louis Begley's previous novels are *Memories of a Marriage, Schmidt Steps Back, Matters of Honor, Shipwreck, Schmidt Delivered, Mistler's Exit, About Schmidt, As Max Saw It, The Man Who Was Late,* and *Wartime Lies,* which won the PEN/ Hemingway award and the Aer/Lingus International Fiction Prize, and was a finalist for the National Book Award. His work has been translated into fourteen languages.

A NOTE ON THE TYPE

This book was set in Hoefler Text, a family of fonts designed
by Jonathan Hoefler, who was born in 1970. First designed
in 1991, Hoefler Text looks to the old-style fonts of the sev-
enteenth century, but it is wholly of its time, employing a
precision and sophistication available only to the late twen-
tieth century.

Typeset by Scribe, Philadelphia, Pennsylvania
Printed and bound by RR Donnelley,
Harrisonburg, Virginia
Designed by Peter A. Andersen